A Friend of America

Written by

Brian Schmit

A Friend of America

The characters, events and places referred to in this book are based on historical facts. However, the story that binds them together, including the personalities and actions of the characters, are fictional. Many of the characters and events are products of the author's imagination and are not intended to resemble actual people or events. When using this book for educational purposes, it is advisable for teachers to consult with the accompanying teachers guide written by Ryan Brech, in accordance with educational standards. This book is a work of historical fiction.

Table of Contents

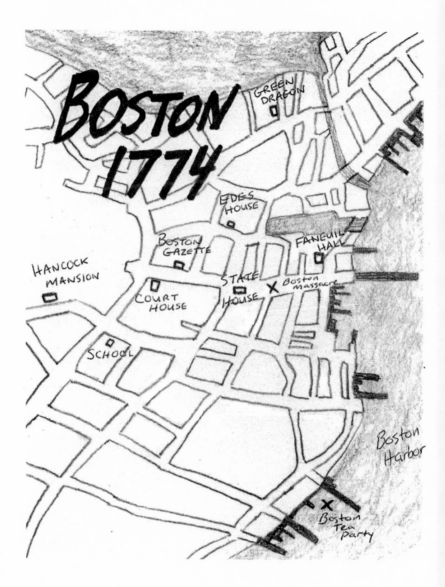

BOSTON 1774

GREEN DRAGON

EDES HOUSE

BOSTON GAZETTE

FANEUIL HALL

HANCOCK MANSION

STATE HOUSE

X Boston Massacre

COURT HOUSE

SCHOOL

Boston Harbor

X Boston Tea Party

1
A Mysterious Plot

On a stormy spring afternoon in New York, Hercules Mulligan heard the familiar sound of bells ringing from the ground floor of his home. Someone had come in the front door of his tailor shop. As he came down the stairs, he saw two men dripping wet just inside his front doorway. One was carrying a set of baggage, no doubt just coming off a passenger ship.

Hercules got quite a few customers from the docks that were just two blocks away. The shop had a good reputation thanks to years of quality work put in by his grandfather who came to America and started the business some thirty years ago. When his grandfather's health began to deteriorate, Hercules's mother thought it would be a good idea for her youngest son to leave Ireland and come to America and help his grandfather. Besides, Hercules had been driving his mother a bit crazy moping around the house all the time.

By coming to America, Hercules could help his grandfather and learn a trade as his apprentice. After three years in America, things had worked out very well. His grandfather appreciated the help, and Hercules actually became a pretty good tailor along the way.

"What can I do for you gentlemen today?" Hercules asked as he reached for a small towel on a chair and handed it to the soggy customers.

The gentleman, without the luggage, took the towel and dried his face.

"My friend here just arrived from London and will be in need of some formal attire for a social gathering."

Hercules always appreciated the business and responded with a friendly smile.

"Well, you've come to the right place." He took each of the men's wet coats and hung them on the coat rack.

"If you follow me to the back room, I'm sure we'll be able to fit you with something to your liking."

Hercules knew exactly what the men were after. Acceptable attire included a white linen shirt, narrow at the arms and shoulders with a slight edge of lace protruding at the cuffs, along with a silk cravat at the neckline. The ensemble would be topped off with a three quarters length coat with turned back cuffs and decorative buttons, all over britches and a waistcoat. Although Hercules had never been to such a formal gala himself, he had learned a lot by listening to his grandfather and other customers. The whole idea behind picking an outfit to wear at a formal affair was to pick something that made you look like you belonged.

As Hercules began to get to work measuring the customer's sleeve length, the two men began chatting with each other. Hercules was always surprised at how he seemed to fade away to the customers once he began fitting them with their clothing, especially when the customers came directly from England. They carried on conversations as if he were nothing more than a piece of furniture.

What hurt Hercules the most was when they wouldn't give a second thought about making derogatory remarks about the Irish right in front of him. The British have always enjoyed putting down the Irish. Ireland was part of the British Kingdom, but it was treated more like a colony. Ireland had long experienced much of the same harsh treatment by the British as America was experiencing now. In fact, as a Catholic back in Ireland, Hercules was not allowed to vote, own land, or practice his religion.

It was Hercules's dream that someday both of his homes, Ireland and America, would gain their independence from the British tyrants. Whenever his British customers would treat him like a second class citizen, Hercules's blood would boil, and he wanted to turn them upside down and mop the floor with their fancy white wigs. But he would always have to bite his lip and keep quiet. It was his grandfather's business, and he knew they couldn't afford to lose any customers.

Today was one such occasion when the two gentlemen seemed to forget he was in the room. After years of listening to conversations he wasn't a part of, Hercules had become pretty adept at figuring out who people were and what their stories were all about.

But on this day, Hercules sensed there was something wrong. He was having a difficult time following their conversation because the two men seemed to be speaking in code. His intuition was telling him that these two guys were up to something.

As Hercules measured the customer for a coat, he listened to the two men talking about their plans. The man who appeared to be from the colonies took out two invitations and flashed them to his friend.

"I've got invitations for the both of us that should work just fine."

Seemed like an odd thing to say about invitations, thought Hercules. *Why wouldn't they work?* Hercules only caught a brief glimpse of the invitations, but one thing he did notice was that the invitations had a picture of a lion standing over a triangle with six crosses on it. He tried to read what the invitations said but could only make out the beginning,

"You are cordially invited."

The conversation between the two men became even more interesting when the tone of their conversation sounded like some kind of underhanded plot. They spoke about *putting an end to this,* and *it's our duty to protect the crown.*

Hercules wondered if he should cough or something to remind the men that he could hear them, but he was becoming too curious about what they were saying, so he stayed silent. At one point, the man getting fitted asked if the other had a list of names.

"I do," the gentleman said, suddenly becoming aware that Hercules was listening to their conversation.

The man paused as if he were considering if Hercules' presence was a problem. Hercules put his head down and held his breath, praying that it was not. After a brief moment, the man gave a look of dismissal towards Hercules as if he were a simpleton who couldn't possibly understand them.

Then he turned back to his friend and in a slightly more guarded manner said, "Let me put it this way, we've decided to *cut the head off the snake.*"

That was the last thing either of them said on the matter. The rest of their time at the shop Hercules tried to maintain a shallow look in his eyes even though his mind was going a million ways trying to figure out what they were up to. The strangers looked at him a number of times as if they were going to interrogate him for his knowledge, but they never said anything.

Once they were finally out the door and on their way, Hercules let out a huge sigh of relief. He went back over to the roll top desk where his grandfather kept the books and took out some paper and a quill. On it he sketched out the symbol he saw at the top of the invitations and tried to write down everything he could remember about the mysterious conversation. He wasn't sure what it all meant, but he knew enough to know that it was important.

Pondering what he had written on the paper, Hercules knew he needed to get to the bottom of this. One characteristic that he developed from his mother growing up in Ireland was a sense of responsibility. Just like when he felt a responsibility to come to America and help his grandfather, he now felt a responsibility to find out what these two men were plotting. He wasn't sure where this would lead, but he knew that the British were up to no good. As an Irishman and as an American, he was going to make sure they were not going to get away with it.

Hercules determined that if he were going to solve this mystery, he was going to need some help, and he knew just the guy for the job. The person he would ask to help him was not only his best friend in America but he was also the smartest guy Hercules had ever met. If there was anyone who could figure out what to do, it was Alexander Hamilton. Hercules decided he would head over to the campus of King's College after work tonight to pay his friend Alex a visit.

2
Burning the Midnight Oil

Bob Sanford had done this routine before. It was after midnight at the Morris Library on the Campus of Kings College, and as usual there was one last lamp flickering on a student's table. Bob had cleaned the entire library, and it was time for him to go home for the evening.

He was tired, hungry, and his thoughts were going back to the smell of the pot roast that had been stewing over the fire the entire day at his house. He wanted to dig into it before he left for the library, but his wife wouldn't let him, saying it wasn't finished. His wife was an excellent cook, and he knew it would be worth the wait. Now the only thing standing between him and that pot roast was this one student with his nose buried deep in a book.

In all the years of working for Kings College, Bob had seen a lot of students come through the library doors. All of them came from very privileged upbringings with bright futures waiting for them when they left. Yet, the young man sitting before Bob was different.   His

8

name was Alexander Hamilton, and he wasn't from America. He was from a small island in the West Indies called Nevis. His mother had raised him on her own, but she passed away leaving him all alone. Unlike the other students who were very wealthy, Alex didn't have a penny to his name.

He did have one thing going for him, however. Alex was brilliant. Growing up in the West Indies, he wasn't allowed into the Catholic school because his parents were not legally married. So he educated himself by devouring every book he could find on the island. He took his first job at fourteen as a clerk at an American trading company on the island of St. Croix. In this job, he became an expert in currencies from around the world and learned how to conduct international business.

He learned so well that, by the age of sixteen, he was put in charge of the entire company. In his spare time, he wrote for the island newspaper and even had an article printed in the New York Times. It was Alex's dream to come to America, and through the help of generous people who recognized his great talents, his passage to America was paid, and he was awarded a scholarship to attend Kings College.

Bob watched this boy, since his arrival just seven months ago, work tirelessly day after day, night after night. His professors could barely keep up with him. When the word got out that Alex was set to earn his bachelor's degree in only one year, the President of the college, Dr. Myles Cooper, asked Alex to slow down to protect the reputation of his college.

Yet Alex had bigger plans. When he was pouring through all those history books back in the West Indies, he learned about the formation of the great societies of Greece, Rome, Egypt, and Persia. He knew then that he wanted to build a modern civilization like those great leaders before him built theirs. For Alex, his destiny was to build America.

So each night when it came time for Bob to tell Alex to go home, he did so with a great deal of trepidation. This seventeen year old prodigy had his sights set far beyond anything Bob could even comprehend. Yet here he was, having to tell the boy genius to quit.

Bob looked across the room at Alex, who seemed to be particularly engrossed in his work tonight. Normally Bob might wait for Alex to look up from his work before asking him to leave. But tonight his wife's pot roast was calling his name. Bob walked over to the table where Alex was working and began sweeping, hoping Alex would get the hint.

No such luck.

Bob decided to cough a few times, but that didn't stir the scholar either.

One last try, Bob thought, and started whistling Yankee Doodle. After about three verses, Bob could see a slight curve forming at the side of Alex's mouth, which slowly relinquished into a full blown smile.

"You know, Bob," Alex interrupted, "the song Yankee Doodle was meant to poke fun at the Americans during the French and Indian War."

Bob had no idea where the tune came from; he just liked to whistle it.

"Is that a fact?" Bob said.

Alex raised his eyebrows and confirmed his statement. "That's a fact."

After a brief moment, the two of them broke into laughter. *That's a fact* was a phrase that had continued through their conversations over the course of the year. Alex loved to tell trivial facts to Bob, and they were always confirmed with the words *that's a fact.* It was a running joke between them that just refused to die.

"You know, Bob, you could just ask me to leave. I won't be upset."

Bob looked at him and nodded his head. "Well, I guess I figure you have a lot more going on in that head of yours than I have reasons to leave."

Alex was taken by the self-deprecation that Bob was exhibiting.

"Something tonight made you resort to whistling a tune to get me out of here. What

11

was this most urgent matter that brought you the courage to interrupt me? Perhaps the lure of riches, maybe power, or was it a beautiful woman?"

Given the choices that Alex presented, Bob felt a bit sheepish to tell him the real reason he wanted to go.

"Well, my dear man what is it?" Alex badgered.

Bob thought for a second more, and then he gave into the pressure.

"Pot roast," he said in a muffled voice.

"Pardon me? Did you just say pot roast?" Alex wasn't expecting to be beat out by a pot roast.

"Not just any pot roast," Bob proudly explained, "but the best pot roast this side of the Atlantic!"

Alex laughed. "Is that a fact?"

Bob raised his eyebrows. "That's a fact."

Alex gathered up his books and let himself out of the library. After walking just one block, he turned around and looked back at the library. Bob was locking the library doors and bounding down the steps heading for home. *That must be one good pot roast,* Alex thought.

It was only three blocks to the college residence hall where he lived. Alex rarely left the campus, a fact he regretted almost daily. There was so much of America that he wanted to see. *All in due time* he kept telling himself.

12

When he got near his residence hall, Alex noticed someone was lying face down on the front steps. Alex very cautiously walked up to the guy, not knowing if he was asleep, injured or dead. Slowly he bent down to get a better look when the body suddenly sprang to life! Alex let out a startled scream and jumped back while the guy on the steps gave a scream of his own. After a heart thumping moment Alex came to his senses, and getting a good look at the guy, recognized his good friend Hercules Mulligan.

3
Ben Franklin's Snake

"Hey, you big oaf!" Alex shouted down at Hercules. "You scared me half to death!"

Hercules rubbed his eyes and looked about, trying to remember where he was. Looking up he saw Alex leaning over him.

"Alex, you're back."

Hercules struggled to his feet and offered a two handed handshake to his good friend.

"It's great to see you, buddy!"

"Yeah, it's good to see you too, Herc." Alex wasn't quite sure what to make of this late night visit.

The two stood there, somewhat awkwardly, while Alex waited for an explanation. Alex could tell Hercules still didn't have his wits about him. Who knows how long he was sleeping there.

"So, what do I owe the pleasure of your visit tonight?" Alex tried to get Hercules focused again.

Hercules thought for a second, and then he remembered.

"Something happened today, and I need to hear what you think about it."

Alex thought it must be pretty important for Hercules to wait to see him so late at night.

"I'd be glad to help in whatever way I can." Hercules was hopeful he would say that.

"Thanks, Alex. I knew I could count on you."

Alex sat down on the stairs with Hercules and listened to his story about the two mysterious men who came into his shop today. Judging from the tone of Hercules voice, Alex knew that the incident unnerved him a bit.

"I think these guys are really out to kill someone." Hercules took out his notes he had folded in his pocket and handed them to Alex.
"I wrote some things down that I thought were clues to what they were up to. Does any of this make any sense to you?"

Alex unfolded the paper and studied it. After a moment, Alex shook his head up and down and said, "I can see why you think that these guys are planning something. It seems suspicious to me as well."

Hercules quickly corrected him.

"It's more than that Alex; I feel it in my gut."

From the look in Hercules eyes, Alex decided to trust his friend's instincts.

"You said that one of the men just came in from London?" Alex inquired.

"That's right, fresh off the boat, his luggage still in hand." Hercules grabbed the air as if he were holding a travel bag.

Alex gave Hercules a serious look. "That guy may be a hired gun."

Hercules' eyes widened as Alex continued with his warning.

"I've seen those types before; they came in whenever there was trouble back home. It's often preferable to use people from out of town to do the dirty work."

Alex had witnessed a lot of underhanded business in the relatively lawless West Indies.

"Those people don't have an emotional attachment to the situation, are not recognizable by the locals, and most of all, they can disappear quickly when they finish the job."

Alex pointed at the paper.

"You wrote here that they said they had to *protect the crown*. That sounds like official government business to me. Just the type of work a hired gun would do."

Hercules was suddenly glad that Alex was helping him, and he wasn't doing this alone. Alex looked a little more at Hercules' notes. He thought the lion over the crosses might be a symbol for some sort of group or club. He knew lions usually stood for strength, but how that was important he didn't know. Of more interest to him was what they said about their target. Alex read aloud off of Hercules's notes.

"They said they were going to *cut the head off the snake.*"

This was definitely something that rang a bell for Alex.

"Herc, come with me up to my room. I want to show you something that I think will shine some light on where these two guys are headed."

Alex led Hercules up the four flights of stairs to the top floor where his room was. It was a hassle to climb up and down the stairs multiple times each day, but Alex thought it was worth it for the peace and quiet. The neighborhood where Kings College was located was one of the toughest in New York. Living on the fourth floor at least got him above the chaos on the street. Another benefit of being on the top floor was that he didn't have anyone above him that was, in essence, walking on his ceiling. None of this, of course, mattered to Hercules, who was huffing and puffing for air by the time he reached the top.

Once inside his room, Alex began looking through his collection of books.

"What exactly are you looking for?" Hercules asked.

"I'm looking for a political cartoon made by Benjamin Franklin just before the French and

Indian War. He printed it in his newspaper, the *Pennsylvania Gazette*, years ago."

Alex had seen it reprinted in one of his textbooks from class. With the incredible volume of work his studies had encompassed this year, it was hard for him to remember exactly which book he saw it in.

"Let me help you look." Hercules offered as he started rifling through the piles of books.

"No, don't bother. I found it."

Alex had the page open and his finger pointed to the drawing.

"Here's the political cartoon of the snake I think your two strangers were referring to."

Alex handed the book over to Hercules and pulled up a chair beside him. Hercules looked at the snake. It was cut in eight pieces and had the words *JOIN, or DIE* underneath it.

"What's so funny about a cut-up snake?"

Alex grabbed the book back.

"It's not supposed to be funny. It's not that kind of cartoon."

Alex put the book back in front of Hercules again. "Listen, Herc, here's what Ben Franklin is trying to say with this political cartoon."

Alex pointed to the different pieces of the snake, each representing different colonies.

"Notice how the snake winds around to symbolize the American coastline."

Hercules didn't know his geography well but took Alex's word for it.

"Okay, I can see that the snake represents the colonies, but what does Franklin mean by *JOIN or DIE?* It sounds threatening."

"Well, I think it was more of a warning than a threat," Alex explained. "When Franklin wrote this, the French were posing a pretty big problem to the British Colonies. Franklin was pointing out that the colonies would be a much stronger force if they were united against the French." Benjamin Franklin later made a formal proposal for unification in the Albany Plan of Union, which was rejected by the colonies.

Alex recalled reading about how Franklin's snake became a popular symbol in the colonies, with many newspapers reprinting the image. Over time the symbolism of the snake switched from encouraging unity against the French to, more recently, a call to unity against the British. Alex pointed to the section of the snake with the head.

"This is where the two strangers are going."

Hercules looked at the N.E. written above the snake's head. "They're headed to New England?"

"More specifically, they're going to Boston."

If the British indeed felt threatened that the colonies might unite against them in a revolution, then the best way to stop them would be to take away their leaders, or metaphorically speaking, *cut off the snake's head.*

"They're going after the leaders of the rebellion in Boston. They're going after the Sons of Liberty."

"We have to stop them!" A suddenly agitated Hercules said, standing up as if he were ready to take on the entire British army himself.

"Hold on there, my friend." Alex grabbed his arm. "We can't just go charging after people who haven't done anything wrong yet."

Hercules didn't see it that way. "Would you rather we wait until someone dies and then live with the guilt that we could have stopped them?"

Alex thought Hercules made a compelling case, but going after the potential culprits by themselves seemed foolish. Alex had another plan.

"Let's go to Boston and warn the Sons of Liberty."

Hercules wanted to do more than just warn them, but he thought that was at least a good start. "We can use my grandpa's buggy. It will give old Betsy a chance to stretch her legs a bit."

"Then it's settled." Alex slapped Hercules on the shoulder. "We'll leave first thing in the morning."

After making a few plans, Hercules left, and Alex thought about what he just agreed to. All his focus since coming to America had been on getting through college. Taking time away from his studies had not been in his plans, but after further consideration, he knew he was doing the right thing. This was the opportunity he had been waiting for. College was a path towards getting opportunities to make his mark in the world. But today one of those opportunities had just showed up at his doorstep. Alex had a chance to be a part of what could be the beginnings of a revolution. This he couldn't pass up.

A smile came across Alex's face as he thought about going to Boston. And he knew just who they needed to see. Ben Edes was the editor of the Boston Gazette and a person Alex greatly admired. Alex wrote articles for his college newspaper and had been following the events in Boston by reading the Gazette, which was delivered to the school every other week. Nobody had a better handle on the pulse of Boston than Ben Edes. He surely would be able to get them started on their quest, and it would be a great honor to actually meet the man in person.

As Alex crawled inside the covers of his bed that night, he had a feeling of calmness come over him. Everything seemed to be coming together. He came to America to be a difference maker, now here was his chance. This was his calling; this was his destiny.

4
A Famous Rider

Alex got up before the dawn, packed a light bag, and headed down to the corner of Broadway and Wall Street to Hercules' tailor shop. This was a prime location where two of New York's busiest streets came together. Grandpa Mulligan had no idea it would be such a good location thirty years ago when he opened the shop. It was just the cheapest real estate he could find at the time. Now thanks to a lot of hard work and a little luck, he built something that he could pass down to his grandson.

Grandpa Mulligan was very proud of Hercules. He not only picked up the skill of tailoring well, he also was a very loving and caring grandson who was a tremendous help to he and his wife as they grew old. It was for that reason that he had no trouble giving Hercules a few days off and the use of his horse and buggy. If anyone deserved it, it was Hercules.

By the time Alex got there, Hercules already had Betsy hitched up and ready to go. After a quick hug and a peck on the cheek from his grandmother, who slipped Hercules a handkerchief full of cookies for the road, the two adventurous young men were off.

It was a two and a half day ride to Boston by horse and buggy. Since Betsy wasn't used to traveling so far, Hercules wasn't about to push her too hard. They would go as far as Betsy would take them each day then camp along the road to rest her. As they left the city of New York, the sun started to peek out from the horizon. Feeling the warmth of the sun on his face and the breeze in his hair, Alex was thankful to get a brief hiatus away from the musty air of the Kings College Library.

The road between New York and Boston was a well-traveled route. Alex and Hercules passed many people going both directions. Most people were on horseback, but there were a few walking as well. There were also a lot of wagons on the road, some with families moving about, but most with traveling salesmen who were taking their products from town to town. Alex and Hercules were making good time with Betsy keeping a steady trot going. They had only stopped a few times to get the horse some water and a short rest. Alex and Hercules were enjoying the trip but were excited to get to Boston.

Most travelers along the road were traveling at a modest place. So when a rider approached them at a full gallop, it caught their attention.

"I wonder why this man is in such a hurry?" Hercules asked as the rider drew closer.

It was a man in his late thirties, and he had a saddlebag that was loaded up and clanking a bit as it bounced on the horse. As he approached, he was yelling something, but they couldn't make out what. Hercules brought the buggy to a halt, and the rider pulled up beside them.

"Where are you boys headed?" he asked, slightly out of breath.

"We're going to Boston" responded Hercules. "Why, what's going on?"

The rider's horse was prancing around as if it were raring to go again. Holding the reigns, the rider told them that British ships had arrived in Boston loaded with redcoat soldiers.

The rider continued while keeping his horse at bay.

"King George is going to take control of Boston after what we did, throwing all his tea into the harbor. If you boys don't have to be in Boston, I would recommend that you turn around and go home."

Hercules was getting a bit offended. That was the second time this man had referred to them as boys, and now he was telling them to go home where it's safe. Hercules was ready to give this dunderhead a piece of his mind when Alex elbowed him in his side and nodded towards the rider's saddlebag. Hercules looked and saw the word *Revere* etched into the leather, which meant nothing to him, but Alex knew who the rider was.

Alex had been following the events taking place in Boston through the New York newspapers. The man most often quoted in the articles was Paul Revere, one of the members of the Sons of Liberty. After the Boston Tea Party, the Sons of Liberty decided to become more organized in preparation for what they knew was coming, a concentrated effort by the King to punish Boston and reassert control. They formed committees of correspondence in each city to conduct meetings and maintain communication. They also started a committee of public safety that had riders pass the news of the British crackdown throughout the colonies. Their best rider was a silversmith from Boston named Paul Revere.

"Are you Paul Revere?" Alex asked knowing full well he was.

"I am. Who are you boys?"

Boys? Hercules had enough. Alex watched as Herc's face turned all red and his neck tightened. Before he knew it, Hercules jumped down from the buggy and was standing tall, with his chest pushed out, in front of Paul Revere's horse.

"I'll show you who I am if you call me boy one more time!"

Alex quickly hopped down and grabbed Hercules, laughing to diffuse the tension.

"What my friend meant to say is that we're headed to Boston because we have urgent news for the Sons of Liberty."

Revere could see that he may have misjudged them.

"My apologies," Revere said, getting down from his horse. "Any man willing to help the cause deserves my respect."

Revere offered his hand. Hercules was looking at the ground determining if he still wanted to slug him. When he decided he did not, he shook Revere's hand. Revere smiled and shook Alex's hand as well.

"So tell me about this urgent news."

Hercules looked over to Alex for some guidance.

"It's alright to tell him. He's with the Sons of Liberty."

Hercules nodded and went on to tell his story about the two mysterious strangers who came into his shop.

Revere was glad that he ran into Alex and Hercules, especially since he could be one of the people the British were targeting.

"You two are right to pass this information on. With what's going on in Boston, it wouldn't surprise me if the British resorted to some underhanded tactics to squash the rebellion."

Alex felt good that their suspicions were being taken seriously by Revere.

"Unfortunately, I'm not going to be able to help you, at least not for a few days."

Revere grabbed his saddle and pulled himself back up on his horse.

"I'm headed to New York to let everyone know that the British troops have landed in Boston, and we will need their support."

Alex knew this was important. If the colonies were going to sustain any sort of effective rebellion, they were going to have to do it together, not separately, just like Ben Franklin warned with his snake drawing *JOIN, or DIE.*

Revere went on, "This can't be only Boston's battle. It needs to be an American battle if we truly want to keep our rights and freedoms."

Alex nodded his agreement.

"Maybe you could help us get started?" Alex asked Revere. "I thought we would begin by informing Ben Edes at the Gazette."

Revere agreed. "Ben's a good man and will be able to guide you to the others."

Revere's horse began to prance again, ready to bolt down the road.

"Try the newspaper print shop on Queen Street in the morning. Otherwise he may be at the Green Dragon Tavern in the afternoon."

The saddlebags began to clank again with the horse dancing around.

"What's clanking in the saddlebag?" Hercules questioned.

Revere pulled out a silver spoon from the bag. "It's just some of my silverware. I need to deliver it to a customer in New York. A man's still got to make a living you know."

Revere put the spoon back in the bag and gave them an appreciative tip of his hat.

"Good luck to you, men. The Sons of Liberty are in your debt."

Revere pulled back on the reins; his horse reared up on his hind legs then took off like a shot down the road, leaving Alex and Hercules in a cloud of dust.

Brushing themselves off, they climbed back on the buggy. Hercules thought for a moment about cracking the reigns and sending Betsy dashing down the road in the same manner as Revere, but he thought he better not risk pushing Betsy too hard. With a quick whistle and a light flick of the reigns, Betsy resumed her trot down the dusty road. It felt to Alex like they had just been deputized to carry out an important mission on behalf of the Sons of Liberty. *This was getting exciting.* Alex thought as they made their way down the road to Boston.

5
Flying Potatoes

After nearly three days on the road, Alex and Hercules reached the town of Boston early in the afternoon. Along the way, they found a couple nice places to camp. One of them had a gently running stream next to it for Betsy to get a drink of water. Alex figured that site had to be one of the more popular places for camping since it had a well-used fire pit and most of the brush around it had been cleared away. It was nice to sleep under the stars and in the fresh air. It reminded Alex of his childhood when he and his friends would camp out on a regular basis.

He must have been awfully tired last night because he had no trouble falling asleep, and he slept soundly the entire night. Unfortunately he woke up with a terribly stiff neck caused by the unfortunate location of a tree root under his head. Alex was rolling his head around in circles, in an attempt to loosen his neck, as Betsy pulled their buggy onto the streets of Boston.

Alex had never been to Boston before. It was a town of about sixteen thousand people,

30

roughly half the size of New York. Alex had read about most of the town being destroyed by a massive fire fourteen years earlier. Fire was always a problem in the colonies. With most buildings being built of wood and having large fireplaces, wood burning stoves, lanterns and candles, it wasn't hard to see the risk. The buildings in towns like Boston were also built very close together to make it easy for citizens to walk from one place to another. The problem was if one building caught on fire, the whole town was likely to go up in flames.

The town of Boston had been the first in the British colonies to thrive. It was located at the mouth of three rivers and had a magnificent harbor, all of which made Boston ideal for trade. Their entire economy was closely tied to trade, especially with London, one of the strongest trading centers in the world. This relationship between the two cities had kept them tethered to each other both economically and emotionally. Unfortunately, over the last ten years of rebellion, a large and visible chasm had been driven between those loyal to England and those patriots caught up in the rebellion.

At first glance, Boston looked like any other town to Alex. Its streets were narrow and crooked, most of them made of dirt, some paved with cobblestones. The citizens shared the streets with livestock, which clogged traffic and left a rather unpleasant odor when the wind wasn't blowing. The majority of people Alex saw walking about were under the age of sixteen, which reflected the general population of the time. The town was alive and bustling, with no visible sign of the hostilities that had gripped the town for so long.

As their buggy got deeper into the heart of the city, that peaceful perception began to change. More and more Alex noticed the presence of the British redcoat soldiers. They were usually stationed in pairs on street corners and in front of public buildings. They didn't look like they were there to help or be of service to anyone; rather they were monitoring the behaviors of the town's people. Every time they rounded a corner there appeared more and more soldiers. By the time they got to the city center, Alex and Hercules looked around in amazement. About one out of every four people they could see was dressed in a red military uniform.

With their mouths hanging open and their eyes as big as saucers, Alex leaned over and whispered to Hercules, "This town is under a military occupancy."

Just then the daze that they had fallen into was awoken by the undeniable sound of Hercules' stomach growling with the force that was almost scary.

"Maybe we should get something to eat," Hercules suggested with a sheepish grin.

Alex was fine with that knowing how irritable Hercules could get when he was hungry.

"Let's see what we can find," Alex smiled. "We wouldn't want these redcoats to arrest you for disturbing the peace."

They rode around for a few more blocks, looking for a place to eat, when they saw a building with a copper dragon above its door. It was the Green Dragon, the tavern where Paul Revere said they might find Ben Edes. Seemed like the perfect place to get some food and start their search. The Green Dragon Tavern was a large three story brick structure located on Union Street on the north side of town. Pulling the buggy up to the tavern, they tied Betsy up on the hitching post and went inside.

Walking through the front door, both Alex and Hercules hesitated.

"Are we in the right place?" asked Hercules.

It seemed like they had entered a public meeting house that had some large meeting rooms on both sides of the building. Scanning the lobby, Alex saw a flight of stairs heading down and a sign hanging on an angle that said *tavern* with an arrow pointing towards the basement. As they walked down the stairs, Hercules was starting to feel a bit claustrophobic. The ceiling was rather low, and there wasn't a whole lot of sunlight coming through the small windows up near the ceiling.

The two of them were able to find their way to an open table in the dimly lit tavern. Once their eyes began to adjust, they could see that the place wasn't actually half bad. There were quite a few people at the Green Dragon, most of them bellied up to the long mahogany bar that ran the entire length of the back wall. There was another grouping of people sitting at tables on the opposite side of the room. Alex and Hercules found an open table between the two groups. There was a good deal of cheer and a generally friendly atmosphere. But most importantly to Hercules, there was the definite aroma of food in the air.

Not wanting to wait too long, Hercules waved his hand and got the attention of the waitress who hurried over.

"What can I do for you boys today?"

Alex prepared himself for Hercules to take exception to being called a boy again. Instead, perhaps because of the apparent hunger emergency, Hercules responded in a quick, decisive manner.

"Whatever that is that I smell, I'll have a plate full."

The waitress laughed. "That would be ham and boiled potatoes."

"Sounds great and hurry if you can."

She gave Hercules a motherly grin. "I'll do my best, sweetheart."

Alex decided to order the same so as to not hold up the process. Then, as promised, in a matter of minutes, the platters of ham and potatoes were in front of them, and all you could see of Hercules was his elbows flaring and the incredibly fast movement of his fork from the plate to his mouth.

As Hercules continued to finish his own plate, Alex could see that he was also eyeing what was on his plate. Always one to help someone in need, Alex pushed his plate across the table to the bottomless pit that was his friend. While he waited for Hercules to devour his second plate of food, Alex struck up a conversation with the waitress to try to find out some information. She looked like a person who knew what was going on.

"Ma'am, do you know a man named Ben Edes?"

The waitress looked at him as if he were crazy.

"Well, first, my name is Sally, and second, of course I know Ben; he comes in here all the time."

Alex probed further. "When did you see him last?"

"He was upstairs yesterday for a meeting with the Sons of Liberty. They were worried about all the British ships that floated into the

35

harbor packed with more redcoats. I think they decided to send Paul Revere to New York to garner some support."

Alex nodded his head as he put the pieces together.

Suddenly, out of the corner of his eye, Alex thought he saw something fly over his head. He started looking around the dark ceiling.

"I think I just saw a bat."

Sally ignored his comment. "Why are you looking for Ben anyway?"

Alex kept looking around as he answered. "We have some information for him, and Paul Revere said we might find him here."

Just then another object went whizzing past in the opposite direction, just missing Hercules.

"What was that?" Hercules yelled, nearly choking on his food.

"Well, it's not a bat," Alex said. "I think it was a pickle."

Sally watched as her two patrons sat with perplexed looks on their faces.

"Let me clue you in on the flying food," Sally said as she pulled up a chair and sat down. She pointed over at the group sitting at the bar.

"Most of those guys are members of the Sons of Liberty. They have regular meetings upstairs with their Committee of Correspondence. They've kind of claimed the tavern as their headquarters."

Alex understood now why Paul Revere told them this would be a good place to find Ben Edes. Sally pointed over in the opposite direction towards the group sitting at the tables.

"Over there are the guys still loyal to the King. The loyalists don't like all this talk of rebellion, and they don't like that their favorite tavern is being used for planning it."

Alex looked back and forth between the two groups. "It looks like we picked a table right in the line of fire."

Alex knew this resentment that was created between the loyalists and the patriots was becoming a huge problem in Boston. Even though he favored the patriots, Alex could see both sides of the argument. Those loyal to the King were part of the Tory political party, which had been around for a long time back in England. Even though they didn't like the King's taxes, the royal family had ruled England for centuries, and whatever they determined to be good for the country needed to be supported by their citizens. The Tories, as they were called, were proud of being from the strongest country in the world and enjoyed the economic and military benefits that being under the King's rule afforded them. Alex could understand why the Tories would want to keep business as usual and remain in good graces with the King.

At the same time, Alex also respected the opinions of the patriots who were leading a rebellion against their own government. Why shouldn't they want representation in the British Parliament? It seemed unfair to have taxes forced upon them when they had no way for their voices to be heard. Since the time the Mayflower first landed in America and the pilgrims wrote the Mayflower Compact, the colonists had been, for the most part, governing themselves through colonial assemblies. The King had always taken an attitude of salutary neglect towards America, allowing them to make their own decisions and do as they saw fit. England and its colonies were three thousand miles apart, and maintaining tight control would simply cost the King too much. Besides, under that system America was thriving.

But now things were different. Since the British came over to help defeat the French in the French and Indian War, they suddenly wanted to start recovering the money they spent on the war by taxing the colonies. Alex could see how the patriots would feel like they were being taken advantage of and used as a source of revenue for the King's profit.

"How do you put up with all this fighting between your customers?" Alex asked Sally.

"As long as it's confined to throwing food and insults at each other, I can manage it."

But Sally had a look on her face that told Alex that it wouldn't remain that way for long.

"Sometimes I feel like I'm sitting on a time bomb just waiting for it to explode."

Alex thought that the British probably felt the same way and that was the reason they sent all those redcoat soldiers to Boston. *They're getting ready for a fight,* thought Alex.

"Sally," Alex leaned over towards her and whispered, "Do you think we're headed for a war?"

Sally looked like she wished she hadn't heard the question, but her eyes told Alex all he needed to know. Before she could utter a word, another projectile came flying in. This time it was way off its intended course and hit Hercules square in the side of the head. *Splat!* It was one of those little boiled potatoes that flew into Hercules and dropped straight down into his glass of water, which splashed up and onto his shirt and lap. Hercules began to stand up and look for the source of the attack.

"What is wrong with you people?" Hercules yelled out.

Seeing the sight of an innocent bystander getting caught in the middle of their food fight caused both sides to laugh in delight. The further humiliation of being laughed at made it even worse for Hercules.

"Well, I'm glad I can be a source of amusement for all of you," Hercules sarcastically yelled while wiping the potato off his face and flicking it on the floor. "Let's get out of here."

Hercules gave one last angry glare at the still laughing crowd, then turned and walked off in a huff. Alex looked over at Sally trying hard to keep himself from laughing as he got up from the table.

"Well, I guess it's time for us to go."

Sally couldn't help but to smile at Hercules's misfortune.

"Good luck in finding Ben. I would try his house over by Brattle Square if I were you."

Alex nodded and waved, as he headed back up the stairs, laughing a little since Hercules couldn't see him.

When he made his way out the door of the Green Dragon and back into the bright sunlight, there sat Hercules already in the buggy, staring straight ahead, trying to recover from the embarrassment. Alex tried to compose himself, keeping the smile off his face. He pulled himself onto the buggy and just sat there staring straight ahead as well. After a few moments, Alex couldn't take it anymore and burst out in laughter. Seeing his best friend so giddy, Hercules had to laugh too but gave Alex a good sock in the arm for laughing first.

6
The Edes Family

It was only a couple of blocks to Brattle Street, where Ben Edes lived, just off the alley. They found Brattle Street by asking someone, and they found the Edes residence by asking someone else. Alex and Hercules tied up Betsy to the fence and made their way to the front door. The front door had one of those fancy brass knockers with the name *EDES* engraved on it. Alex reached up, grabbed the handle, and knocked three times. After a bit of a wait, the door appeared to open magically in front of them without anybody standing before them. Then Alex felt a tug on his pant leg. He looked down and saw a small boy around the age of four, with blue eyes and a big toothy smile, staring up at him.

"Well, hello there, my name is Alex, and this is my friend Hercules. We're here to see your father."

The little boy just looked at them, giggled, and slammed the door. Hercules gave Alex a look of bewilderment.

"First, I'm hit with a potato and now this. I'm starting to get the idea that they don't like us in Boston."

Alex smiled. "Don't take it personally; I'm sure he was just having fun."

A moment later the door opened again. This time it was a middle aged lady wearing an apron and holding the little boy on her hip.

"Good afternoon, Ma'am. My name is Alex, and this is Hercules. We've come from New York to see Ben Edes."

The lady smiled and moved aside opening the door wide.

"Well, you're at the right place. Come on in, and make sure you wipe your feet. I just finished the floors, and I'd like them to stay clean for at least a little while."

Alex and Hercules wiped their feet on the front door mat and walked in. There was a flurry of activity at the Edes house. It seemed everywhere they looked there was a kid running around. It was like they walked into a schoolhouse during playtime. Mrs. Edes looked around at all the kids, set the little boy down on the floor, and cupped both hands around her mouth to project her voice.

"Alright, everybody outside!" she called out.

The kids started scrambling every which way with Mrs. Edes right behind them picking things up as they left the room.

42

"I have ten kids, but I'm not exactly sure who all those kids are to tell the truth."

Martha and Ben had been married for twenty years. They were a couple that complimented each other perfectly. Her strengths were his weaknesses and vice versa. Neither one of them could imagine life without the other. Martha attempted to fix her hair, which was a bit frazzled from the daily happenings of the household.

"If you wait one moment, I'll see if Ben can come down and see you."

Martha went up the stairs with the little boy trailing behind her. As soon as she was gone, the door opened from behind them, and a teenage boy in a jacket and wearing a large brimmed hat walked in. He shoved his way right between the two of them and over to the hallway table where he sat down a satchel and started unpacking it.

Alex and Hercules stood patiently at the door waiting for Ben Edes to come down. The house that was previously a whirlwind of activity was now peaceful with nobody around but the boy at the table. After about five minutes, there was finally some noise from upstairs. A man came walking down the stairs with reading glasses on his head and rolling his shirt's sleeves up to his forearms.

"You must be my visitors." The man said as he reached the bottom of the stairs. "I'm Ben Edes."

He reached out to shake their hands. Alex instantly liked Ben and shook his hand enthusiastically. Having written for his hometown newspaper as well as his school newspaper, Alex had a deep admiration for Ben and his work with the Boston Gazette.

"We really appreciate you meeting with us," Alex said smiling ear to ear.

"It's my pleasure, but I'm curious as to what would bring someone all the way from New York to see me."

Ben moved towards the parlor motioning for his guests to follow him. Before they left into the next room, Ben called out.

"Maggie, could you please bring some glasses of lemonade into the parlor for our guests?"

Alex and Hercules looked around and then at each other. *Who was he talking to*? They wondered. Then the teenager at the hallway table stood up and took off her coat and hat, allowing her long blonde hair to flow down her shoulders. Alex nearly fell over. He stood there staring, not able to believe his eyes. Seemingly, out of nowhere, a beautiful girl had magically appeared before them. Alex was lost in a trance. Hercules grabbed his buddy's sleeve and pulled him into the parlor.

Ben sat down on one of the chairs while Alex and Hercules sat down on the couch.

"So, what do I owe the pleasure of your visit?" asked Ben.

Hoping to give them some credibility, Alex brought up that they ran into Paul Revere, who told them to come here. Ben wasn't too impressed, so Alex decided to cut to the chase.

"We believe that there is going to be an attack on the leaders of the Sons of Liberty."

Ben sat up in his chair and was obviously interested. Alex went on to explain the whole story to Ben. He told them about Franklin's snake metaphor, and he let Hercules tell his part about seeing the invitations.

None of it seemed to surprise Ben. There was no doubt that King George was angered with the colonies and determined to put an end to further rebellious activity. King George knew that the main source of the rebellion was coming from the Sons of Liberty. When the Sons of Liberty had the audacity to throw his tea into Boston Harbor, it was the final straw. The King responded by instructing Parliament to pass the Coercive Acts, or the Intolerable Acts as the patriots liked to call them.

The purpose of the Acts was to punish the Sons of Liberty and bring the colonies back in line. In direct response to the Sons of Liberty dumping their tea in the harbor, the Intolerable Acts completely shut down the harbor to all trade. This greatly affected most of the merchants of Boston, who were, not coincidently, members of the Sons of Liberty.

Another measure of the Intolerable Acts meant to curtail the activities of the Sons of Liberty was the ban on town meetings. Any town meetings not approved by the Governor were now outlawed. This was a blatant attempt at stopping the Sons of Liberty from meeting in their Committees of Correspondence. To get around the law, the meetings were no longer posted to the public but kept secret by the members of the Sons of Liberty. Sam Adams made the Green Dragon their primary meeting place, making it difficult for law enforcement to know if they were at the tavern for socializing or for planned meetings. Given all that was happening in Boston, the fact that the King might be trying to place an attack on the leadership of the Sons of Liberty was no surprise to Ben Edes. The questions Ben had were when and where?

The door of the parlor opened. Maggie was backing through it with both hands on a tray of lemonade trying to keep it steady. Alex quickly jumped up and came to her aid grabbing a hold of the tray.

"Let me help you with that," he smiled at Maggie as he took the tray from her.

"Oh, thank you," Maggie replied, a bit flustered by the obvious attention Alex was giving her. Hercules lowered his head and shook it back and forth in disgust. Alex couldn't take his eyes off her as he clumsily put the tray down nearly spilling the drinks. Maggie looked like a totally different person than when Alex saw her just a few minutes ago. She had strawberry blonde hair and cute little freckles on her nose. Her eyes were blue, and when she smiled at Alex, dimples emerged on each cheek. Alex kept standing, waiting like a gentleman for Maggie to have a seat. Maggie wasn't clued in on this, however, and continued to move about the room. Although her features were very feminine, she moved like a tomboy, and you could tell she would be much more comfortable throwing rocks than picking flowers.

Ben could see what was going on and attempted to get Alex's mind back to business and off his daughter.

"So you mentioned that those two mysterious men had invitations to a gathering of some sort."

Alex nodded as he sat back down.

"That's right," trying to refocus, Alex looked at Hercules. "Show Mr. Edes what you wrote down about the invitations."

Hercules started fishing through his pockets for the paper he wrote on. Finding it, he unfolded the crumpled paper for Ben. On the paper was the sketch that he made of the lion on top of the crosses. Immediately upon seeing it, Ben knew exactly what it was.

"If this is what I think it is, we know where they are going to be."

Alex and Hercules leaned in to take another look at the drawing.

"Maggie, could you go to my desk and bring down the Adams invitation in the top drawer?"

Alex, who was still struggling to keep his eyes off Maggie, watched her as she left the room. When Maggie took a peek back over her shoulder, Alex quickly looked away causing Maggie to smile.

"So what do you think this is?" Hercules asked pointing to the design he sketched on the paper.

Ben looked a little closer. "I'm pretty sure this is the coat of arms of John Adams. I've seen it a few times on different items of his."

Hercules wasn't exactly sure what a coat of arms was, but he didn't want to seem ignorant by asking. Instead, he remembered a trick he learned from his grandfather. When you want more information, just repeat whatever someone says back to him, and then it's only natural for him to clarify what he said.

"The coat of arms of John Adams." Hercules repeated.

"Yes." Ben replied. There was a slight pause; then Ben began to explain further like Hercules had hoped.

"The practice started over five hundred years ago when knights painted their shields different colors before going into battle. The custom evolved over the years as nobles added symbols, depicting their family heritage, to their coat of arms. They put it on everything from tapestry to silverware."

Ben tilted the paper so Hercules could see. "This triangle you drew is actually a shield which represents the original shield of the knights. Everything on the shield symbolizes something about the family."

Hercules was fascinated by this. "What does the lion and all of those crosses mean?"

"Lions usually represent strength or courage, and these crosses, which also look like swords, symbolize an undeniable faith."

Hercules took the drawing and started thinking about what his family coat of arms would be like. His thoughts carried him away, and he wondered if he could make his own coat of arms for his family and put it up in his tailor shop back in New York.

"I bet I could stitch one of these for my grandparents." Hercules enthusiastically told Alex.

It always put a smile on Alex's face when his friend got so excited about the simplest things. He wished that sometimes his mind wasn't so bogged down with so many complexities that he could enjoy some of the little things in life, like Hercules did.

When Maggie came back into the room she was carrying a single white card in her hand.

"Is this what you wanted?" she asked handing her father the card.

"Yes, thank you Maggie." Ben took the invitation and looked at it. "Is this the invitation the two strangers had?"

Ben handed the invitation to Hercules whose expression told the answer as soon as he saw it.

"Absolutely!"

Looking over the coat of arms at the top of the invitation, Hercules was proud that his idea to make a quick drawing of what he saw that day lead them to find this. Alex grabbed the invitation from Hercules and studied it. He turned the invitation over where a larger version of the crest was with the name of John Adams directly under it.

John Adams

"Sure enough, the crest of John Adams." Alex said flipping the invitation back over. "It says here that the party is tomorrow night at the home of John Hancock."

Hercules, still fixated on the coat of arms asked, "Why would the Adams coat of arms be on the invitation if the party is at John Hancock's house?"

Ben understood Hercules' confusion. What Hercules didn't know was that the Hancock residence was actually the site of numerous parties, many of which were not his own.

"John Hancock is one of the wealthiest men in Boston, and his home is an elegant mansion, one of the finest in the area."

Alex noticed Maggie's excitement when her father spoke of the Hancock mansion. Ben continued to explain,

"I have no doubt that he graciously offered his home to the Adams' for their party. The Adams' live more than ten miles outside of town, and their home is not nearly as suitable for entertaining."

Sorting all this information in his head, Alex knew they needed to find out more about this party and who was going to be there.

"We're going to need to find John Adams and talk to him about his party."

Ben laughed. "I agree you need to find out the details of this party, but it's not John you need to talk to."

Alex was confused. "I thought you just said that it was an Adams party?"

Ben shook his head. "I did, but John won't know anything more than where the party is and when he has to be there."

"Well then, who do we talk to?" Alex asked."

Out of the corner of the room, Maggie spoke up. "Abigail."

Alex turned to face Maggie.

"It's Abigail's party. In fact, I'm supposed to help her set up tomorrow. I could take you with me if you want to go."

Alex was temporarily stunned by this question.

Seeing his tongue-tied friend frozen, Hercules responded for him. "That would be great."

Alex, trying to recover so he didn't seem like a complete idiot, chimed in. "That's nice of you to help us."

Maggie smiled. Ben stood up and summed it up.

"It's settled then. Maggie, will take you to meet Abigail tomorrow, and it probably would be a good idea to get the word to Sam Adams and John Hancock as well. Those two are probably on top of any list the King may have."

Alex and Hercules were more than willing to speak to anyone Ben suggested.

"In the meantime, you'll be my guests tonight. Maggie will show you to the guest room, and you're more than welcome to join us for dinner."

Alex and Hercules jumped to their feet and thanked Mr. Edes for his hospitality.

"Don't mention it," Ben said. "You men are doing a great service to the Sons of Liberty by coming here with this information. It is we who should be thanking you."

Ben shook both their hands as he left the room. Alex felt honored that someone he had admired so much would be so gracious towards them. But then his focus quickly turned back towards Maggie as she was starting out the other door. He watched her as she stopped and turned around, flashed a big smile, tilting her head a little, and asked, "Could you guys help me out with something? It won't take long."

Hercules started to decline the offer so they could check out the town more, when Alex interrupted him.

"We'd be happy to help out in any way we can." He said, smiling back at Maggie.

Hercules was left just shaking his head at Alex's sudden change of priorities.

7

Hercules versus the Chickens

Alex and Hercules followed Maggie outside to the backyard. It was a large yard with a fence around the border. About half of it was covered in grass and the other half was dirt. The yard had a clothesline running through it with sheets blowing in the light breeze. The featured attraction, and undoubtedly the probable reason Maggie brought them back there, was the existence of a chicken coup and a few dozen chickens scattered about the yard.

"Let me guess," Alex said, "this is our dinner."

Picking up a hatchet from the ground, Maggie smirked, "Aren't you the smart one."

She walked over to a log with four spikes nailed on top and drove the hatchet into the wood so that it stuck.

"I'll do the chopping; you two just need to pick out a couple of nice ones."

Alex walked around a little, sizing up the chickens. It didn't take long for him to sneak up from behind on a medium sized chicken and snatch it up into his hands.

"You call that a chicken?" remarked Hercules. "There's barely enough there for me to eat."

Alex felt a little embarrassed that Hercules was showing him up in front of Maggie.

"If you think you can do better, let's see it, big man."

Alex laid down the challenge. Hercules pushed up his sleeves, cracked his back, rolled his neck, and took a deep breath.

"Now, watch how it's done."

Hercules scanned the yard for the biggest chicken he could find. There it was standing about ten feet from him. The only problem, the chicken saw Hercules at the same time Hercules saw the chicken. It was like watching a showdown with both sides waiting to see who would move first. Finally, Hercules started running towards the chicken as fast as he could. The chicken, in turn, tried to fly like chickens do – propelling itself only a foot off the ground and ten feet in the other direction, but it hit the ground running. Hercules was in hot pursuit of the chicken, chasing it all around the yard. A cloud of dust rose up every time the chicken made a quick direction change, and the lumbering Hercules slid in the dirt to change directions and continue the chase. He got close a couple of times when it was running along the fence line, but he ended up with only a few feathers in his hand.

Barreling up the center of the yard, his head down and closing in on the chicken, Hercules never saw it coming when he ran straight into one of the sheets hanging from the clothesline. He stood up, struggling to get the sheet off himself, as Alex and Maggie howled with laughter at Hercules's misfortune. As Hercules finally got the sheet off his head, he noticed Maggie slowly backing the chicken down into the corner and calmly picking it up.

"That's how it's done," she said with a sly smile.

Hercules threw the sheet back over the clothesline.

"I must have tired it out for you."

His face was all red and sweaty, and his chest was heaving up and down as he tried to catch his breath. Maggie and Alex just laughed.

Once the chickens were caught, Alex knew how the process of preparing a chicken went. First, the head and feet had to come off, and then it needed to be cleaned, soaked, and plucked. The last part was the worst; it always took a while to pluck a chicken, but what every boy knew was the first part could be rather amusing. Hercules went over and grabbed the big chicken from Maggie, who put her foot on the log and leaned back to pull the hatchet out.

"Alright, who's first?" She asked while twirling the hatchet in her hands.

Alex started walking forward when Hercules put out his arm to stop him.

"Hold on, I'm not about to let the little book worm here get the last laugh."

Alex stopped and listened to what Hercules had in mind.

"Let's say we bet on whose chicken stays on its feet the longest, my chicken versus your scrawny little bird."

Alex liked the thinking of his always entertaining friend.

"You're on! Prepare to be humiliated."

A look of determination came over Hercules's face.

"Winner gets to choose his prize?"

Alex nodded acceptance.

"And to show you I'm a generous man, I'll let my chicken face the chopping block first."

"You're quite the gentleman," responded Hercules looking anxious to redeem himself after the chicken chasing debacle.

Maggie stood there waiting and enjoying the competition being played out before her.

"Alright contestants, the last chicken to remain standing is the winner."

After twirling the chicken in circles, Alex bent over and put the chicken's neck between the spikes, and with one swift "swumph," Maggie lowered the hatchet sending the head one direction and the body the other. Quickly, so as not to get an unfair advantage, Hercules put his chicken in position, and "swumph" the other chicken was headless.

Both chickens were moving about the yard acting on nerve impulses and muscle memory. They usually could operate in this manner for only about a minute or so. Alex and Hercules each began cheering for their chicken to keep moving and not fall over. Around they walked, the two chickens without their heads. They bumped into everything, but both continued to move around. It was a hilarious site to see. Maggie was getting as much enjoyment out of watching Alex and Hercules scream encouragement at their chickens as she was from the comedy of the chickens running square into each other.

Finally, Alex's chicken seemed to be losing speed. Hercules raised his hands in victory as Alex's chicken wobbled around like a prizefighter going down for the count. The chicken slowly moved into the middle of a group of chickens then, surprisingly, just stopped. Everyone watched for the chicken to fall over, but it was being held up between two other chickens. Hercules started screaming foul play.

"That chicken is being held up by the other chickens!"

Hercules was jumping up and down pointing at the injustice. Just then his chicken began to slow. It teetered to the left a bit, then back to the right, and finally collapsed into the dirt.

"The winner!" Maggie yelled grabbing Alex's hand and holding it in the air in triumph.

"What?" Hercules protested. "Those other chickens were helping Alex's scrawny chicken," Hercules pleaded to deaf ears. "It's a chicken conspiracy I tell you!"

Alex and Maggie were laughing so hard tears came to their eyes. Hercules kicked at the dirt in disgust.

"Stupid chickens!" Hercules mumbled to himself.

He ran over to the group of chickens, waved his arms and shooed them away so that Alex's chicken could finally fall. With the chicken lying in the dirt in front of him, Hercules looked over at Alex; with tongue in cheek and a smile on his face said, "I don't know how you did it, Alex, but somehow you got those chickens to help you."

Alex raised his hands and shrugged his shoulders. "Balancing chickens and flying potatoes, they're all on my side."

Alex motioned to Hercules.

"Come on, grab that winning chicken. We need to clean them up so we can have dinner."

Hercules picked up the chicken and laughed it off. *It's just not my day,* he thought.

8
Dinner Discussion

Dinnertime arrived with a seven year old girl running around the house yelling, "It's time to eat, it's time to eat!"

Between the time Alex and Hercules first entered the dining room until the time they took their seats, the table went from completely empty to completely full. It was a long oak table that could seat fourteen, which it did tonight. With all the children seated, and Mrs. Edes placing the last of the food on the table, Ben walked in, and everyone began to settle down. Seated at the head of the table, Ben cleared his throat, and everyone got quiet and bowed their heads.

"Dear lord, we thank you for the food you have bestowed upon us tonight. We pray that you watch over our guests as they look to help our town and keep us from harm. We thank you for all your gifts, and we praise you for your glory, amen."

As soon as the prayer was over, there was a momentary pause followed by a flurry of activity like Alex had never seen before at the dinner table. Having never been at a table with

61

such a large family, Alex was unaware of the existing rule, survival of the fittest. Everyone was reaching for the food, passing dishes around, and pouring drinks. It was a well-orchestrated routine that was happening at a dizzying pace. Corn going one way, peas the other, chicken disappearing, and an occasional roll tossed across the table.

Alex and Hercules just sat in amazement at the spectacle. Seeing their hesitation, Ben offered some advice to his guests.

"If you don't get it quickly, there won't be any left."

That's all Hercules needed to hear. Diving in with no inhibitions, he used the technique of holding his plate in one hand, hovering over the table, and randomly scooping anything and everything onto his plate with the other. He was a natural in his element. There was a brief pause in the action as Hercules' bravado caught everyone by surprise. Alex, always the gentleman, waited for whatever food was passed around, still managing to adequately fill his plate.

Dinner was a happy occasion at the Edes house. It was a chance to share stories from the day and make plans for tomorrow. A lot of the conversation was about all the redcoat soldiers that had arrived in town.

"It seems like there are more of them than there are of us," remarked one of the kids.

Alex had to ask Mr. Edes his opinion. "What do you think will come of the increased military presence in Boston?"

Ben washed down his food with a sip of cider. "I can't imagine how any good will come of it. For instance, those five men that were shot by the redcoats never would have been shot if the redcoats weren't there trying to break up the crowd in the first place. People should be allowed to assemble without a musket being pointed in their direction."

Ben continued as Alex listened like a student listening to a professor. "Now with so many of them clogging our streets, people are going to get real quiet. Everybody will be worried that if they say anything bad about the government, one of the redcoats will get wind of it, and they'll find themselves in trouble with the law. For no reason other than that they spoke their mind."

Maggie, who was listening in on the conversation, was worried about her father. She had heard people talking around town about how the *Boston Gazette* had articles that questioned the government.

"Could you get in trouble for writing something in the paper?"

Ben looked at his daughter and tried to play if off so as not to worry her. "Well, it seems like there's a little more latitude given to the press ever since the John Peter Zenger trial."

The little four year old, who answered the door when Alex and Hercules fist arrived, recognized that name.

"John Peter is JP's name," he said with that same mischievous smile he had at the door.

Maggie acknowledged her young brother's sharp wit. "You're right, Bobby. That is what JP's name stands for."

Little Bobby beamed with a prideful smile.

Having a lifelong love for the newspaper, Ben had named his first son after John Peter Zenger, a true hero to all American journalists. JP was sitting at the other end of the table. Ben pointed down towards him.

"Tomorrow I'll send JP with you. He'll be able to help you find John Hancock and Sam Adams."

Alex felt like the forces were lining up for them to see all the right people. Alex was especially looking forward to meeting Sam Adams. He knew that Adams was the driving force behind the Sons of Liberty and was excited to learn more about him.

"Have the Sons of Liberty ever made any direct appeals to the government to keep our freedoms from being infringed upon?" Alex asked Ben.

"Of course," Ben replied. "We've written petitions to the Governor and to the King himself, but every time we do so, we are met with hostilities and accusations of sedition."

Alex understood Ben's frustration. If they didn't have a seat in British Parliament and there was no consideration given to their petitions, then how were the citizens' thoughts and concerns to be heard? A government that did not allow for a channel of correspondence with their citizens belonged in a medieval feudal society not a modern day republic.

Alex was enjoying his time with the Edes family. Without his father around and his mother passing away, Alex was always envious of people with large families. In just the brief time they were sitting around the dinner table, Alex picked up on the caring manner in which the family operated. He watched as the older kids helped the younger ones. He saw how the kids showed respect to their mother and father, who in turn listened to their stories and watched after their wellbeing. Even with a few instances of bickering and a couple of bouts of teasing here and there, the family thrived on their interdependency, each of them being better off because of it. Looking back over at Mr. Edes sitting at the head of the table, Alex now understood what Ben and the Sons of Liberty were fighting for.

9
The Minutemen

Alex was getting full and started wondering if he should leave room for the apple pie whose tantalizing aroma had filled the house this afternoon. Hercules had devoured everything in sight and was chatting with the family as if he had known them all his life. With his fork still in his hand, there was no question as to whether Hercules still had room for the apple pie.

Just as Mrs. Edes started to get up from the table to retrieve the pie, there came the sound of a bell ringing. Alex thought it sounded like a school bell, but that didn't make sense given the time of day. Looking around at everyone's worried faces, Alex knew that something was happening. Ben wiped his hands with his napkin and stood up.

"Get the Musket and pistol JP; I'll meet you out front!"

JP took off immediately, nearly tripping as he tried to get up from the crowded table too quickly.

"What's going on?" Alex asked to anyone who would answer.

66

"It's a call for the minutemen." Maggie said with a look of concern in her eyes. "They're a group of townsmen who are willing to respond on a moment's notice to any trouble."

"Like a militia?" Alex asked

"That's right," responded Maggie.

Alex wondered what could be going on that the minutemen were being called tonight. Just then he watched JP bolting down the staircase, musket in one hand, pistol in the other. Ben was holding the front door open for JP, who handed the pistol to him as he hurried out the door. Pulling the door shut behind them, the two volunteer minutemen were gone in an instant. Alex looked over at Hercules who looked over at Alex.

"Well, what are we waiting for?" asked Alex.

Hercules walked quickly to the front door with Alex close behind, turned his head momentarily to thank Mrs. Edes for dinner. Once out the door, they saw Ben and JP about a half block ahead of them and ran to catch up.

As they walked through the streets of Boston, they saw other men coming out of their homes responding to the call of the school bell. The redcoat soldiers stationed at their posts were looking around as if they were wondering what they should do or if they were going to get some orders to move. After about three blocks, they rounded a corner onto School Street, and Alex could see the schoolhouse, which already had about twenty men standing there with guns in hand ready for action. With more men streaming in from all directions, it had the feeling of a battle starting. Alex's heart started to race as they drew closer to the gathering.

The minutemen were all talking to each other about being called together when a man jumped up on a tree stump.

"What's going on, Sam?" Someone from the crowd yelled out.

Alex figured that the man on the stump had to be the famed leader of the Sons of Liberty, Samuel Adams. A hush came over the crowd as they awaited his answer.

"As you are all aware, with the arrival of British ships in our harbor, we have undergone some interesting developments over the last few days. Since I have no doubt that the passengers on those British ships will be coming upon us in a matter of minutes, I'll get right to the point."

Alex looked up the street and saw that the redcoats appeared to be getting organized just as Samuel Adams said.

"Yesterday, three of our members were held for questioning about a recent tar and feathering of a tax collector. While I fully expect our people to be primary suspects and to be questioned in such matters, what I didn't expect was that all three men had their guns confiscated from their homes."

The crowd started jeering and pumping their guns up in the air. Samuel Adams motioned with his hands for them to settle back down.

"It is my opinion that this may be a larger tactic of the redcoat soldiers to disarm the Sons of Liberty."

Alex looked down the street again to see that an equally large crowd of redcoat soldiers were now gathered on the next block and fixing bayonets to their muskets.

"For this reason, I believe we should start to stockpile our weapons for safe keeping."

One of the minutemen yelled out. "I'm not giving up my gun to any redcoat or even to you Sam!"

Many in the crowd shouted their agreement. Samuel Adams answered back.

"George, I'm not trying to take your weapon; everyone needs to keep themselves and their family safe. What I'm trying to do is to ensure that the minutemen and the Sons of Liberty have that same capability."

The crowd was listening.

"What I propose is that each of you keeps a gun for yourselves, and then we'll store away any additional guns you may have, just to be safe."

Alex noticed that the redcoats were now organized in rows and had started marching towards them. It didn't look like Samuel Adams realized that the redcoats were approaching. Alex raised his hand up and started waving it and pointing towards the redcoats. Fortunately, he was able to get the attention of Samuel Adams, who looked down the street and saw the redcoats coming.

"Listen men," Adams yelled, "I have secured a location to store the weapons about ten miles outside of town in Concord. Any extra guns that you can spare should be given to me or John Hancock in the next few days so that we can hide them."

The redcoats were nearly upon them.

"Keep out of harm's way, men; this may only be the beginning!"

Then, just as the redcoats came upon them, the minutemen broke up their meeting and quickly scattered in a dozen different directions. Alex wanted to take the opportunity to speak to Samuel Adams and to warn him about the possible attack at tomorrow's party. With the crowd scurrying all around him, Alex weaved between the minutemen, trying to keep from getting run over, while at the same time keeping Samuel Adams in his sights.

He yelled, "Mr. Adams!" as Samuel Adams jumped up onto his horse. "Mr. Adams, I need to speak with you!"

It was obvious that this wasn't the time, but Samuel Adams recognized Alex as the guy that warned him of the approaching redcoats and yelled back to Alex.

"Come see me tomorrow at the State House!"

Then, he snapped the reins of his horse and galloped off. In the chaos, Alex lost track of Hercules, Ben, and JP. Looking out over the crowd, he saw the redcoat soldiers taking some of the minutemen into custody. Suddenly, Alex felt a firm hand grab on to the back of his collar. Spinning around, expecting to see a redcoat soldier, Alex saw Hercules instead.

"Come on, Alex, we need to get out of here!" yelled Hercules, pulling Alex by his shirt.

Alex followed Hercules, who was clearing the way quite effectively. When they broke into the open, they began to run. Ben and JP were waiting for them about a block away.

Ben was talking with JP about what had just occurred.

"I know people don't want to give up their guns, but if Sam doesn't take them, the redcoats will, and if we lose the ability to form an armed militia, we'll have no way to defend ourselves from the British army."

Alex was surprised at how fast things were progressing in Boston. Plans to stockpile weapons put the dispute between the colonies and the British government at a whole new level. He wondered if the rest of the colonies knew that all this was going on. There were some protests in New York and political unrest throughout the colonies, but in Boston it seemed like they were on the cusp of a war.

10
Unwelcomed Guests

Ben, JP, Hercules, and Alex were walking back to the Edes house when Ben suddenly stopped in his tracks. From the top of the hill on Brattle Street, Ben could look down the hill and see his house. And what he saw was a sight that greatly concerned him. Ever since the boats filled with redcoat soldiers arrived in Boston harbor, Ben knew there would be a chance that this could happen. At the bottom of the hill, standing with her hands on her hips, was Martha Edes defending her home.

In complete disbelief, Martha stood before two redcoat soldiers, pleading with them to leave. She had heard of the Quartering Act back when there was a shortage of barracks for the British Soldiers during the fighting of the French and Indian War. The Act allowed for soldiers to stay in barns, stables, or unoccupied buildings while in America, but the war was long over, and the Act had been repealed. Martha could not understand why these soldiers wanted to take up residency in her home. With ten children, there was no way that she was going to allow that to happen.

73

As Ben drew closer and saw the two soldiers each loaded down with full gear on their backs, he had a good idea why they were there but was hoping it was for something different. When Martha saw Ben and the boys, she looked straight at the soldiers and spoke in her most menacing voice.

"We'll see what my husband has to say about this."

Ben could see the anger in his wife's face and knew he had to be supportive of whatever she wanted, but he feared there was nothing he could do.

"What is the meaning of this?" Ben asked the soldiers as he walked up to them.

Martha couldn't resist telling him first.

"They actually want to bunk here as if we are the new barracks for the British Army."

The two soldiers were not at all sympathetic towards Mrs. Edes' situation. In fact, they seemed to take a bit of pleasure from the imposition they were causing. With a smugness engrained in his face, one of the soldiers turned to Ben and told him, "We have orders to bunk at this residence until further notice."

The other soldier took out two sheets of paper and held them out for Ben to see. Ben knew that it was never a good sign when someone offered up written proof before even being asked for it. Ben took the papers and read them. One was the military orders and confirmed what the soldiers had claimed. The other paper was a copy of the Quartering Act. Martha was right in that the original Quartering Act of 1765 had been repealed. This was the Quartering Act of 1774, however, which was part of the newly enacted Coercive Acts. The only difference between this Act and the earlier Act was this time soldiers were allowed to stay in the colonists homes, even ones that were occupied.

When Ben finished inspecting the papers, a look of submission came over him. He turned to Martha, who knew her husband and knew what he was going to say.

"It's going to be alright, Martha."

Ben had said those words to her whenever they were presented with an obstacle in their lives, and, he was always right. They were always all right, and they would be again when this was all over. Ben gave the papers back to the soldier.

"Everything looks in order."

The soldiers appeared to be enjoying the moment a little too much for Ben's taste, but the last thing he was going to do was to make enemies of people who were going to be staying under the same roof as his family. Ben held his tongue, but Martha, who was already staring fire at the soldiers, wasn't so cordial.

"Of all the homes in Boston, you pick a home that is already bursting at the seams with ten children. You should be ashamed of yourselves."

The soldiers didn't react to the chiding by Mrs. Edes.

"How can they not see the absurdity of what they're doing?" Martha asked her husband.

Ben noticed the soldiers didn't react when Martha pointed out how ridiculous it was to choose their house. This told him one thing. *They knew exactly what they were doing.*

"They're not here because they like being in a house full of children," Ben pointed out. "They're here to keep an eye on the editor of the local newspaper."

The two soldiers took a quick glance at each other. Ben took the lack of a denial from the soldiers as confirmation that he was right.

"Nevertheless, they are our guests and we'll treat them as such." Ben put his hand on JP's shoulder. "My son will show you to your room."

JP opened the door for the soldiers, who walked into a home where they weren't welcome.

"I'm not cooking for them," Martha declared, trying to assert some control in the matter.

Ben felt like he let Martha down and wished he could have done something to stop them.

"You don't have to give them anything more than what the law requires; bedding, candles, cider, and salt."

That didn't change Martha's contempt for the situation much, but she was going to do what she had to do. Martha looked around and noticed that the neighbors had been watching the activities at their house. They were probably thankful the soldiers came to her house instead of theirs. Composing herself, Martha straightened her apron, stiffened her lip, and went back inside.

Alex and Hercules stayed out of the way during the Edes' confrontation with the redcoats, but having just watched their room being taken from them, they were wondering where they'd sleep tonight. Ben wasn't about to leave them without a place to stay.

"Don't worry, I haven't forgotten about you." Ben reassured them. "There's a couch and a cot in the back office of the Boston Gazette. You're more than welcome to stay there for the night."

Alex and Hercules were grateful once again for Mr. Edes' continued hospitality.

"I'll have to tell my partner John Gill, so he won't be startled when he comes in the morning and finds you."

After going back inside and finishing a piece of apple pie, JP took them over to the offices of the Gazette. They put Betsy in the back stable where Hercules was able to tend to her horseshoes, which seemed to be bothering her after the long trip. Alex found some hay for her to eat and water to drink. Going inside the print shop and looking around, it was a lot smaller than Alex had imagined. It wasn't much bigger than what Kings College had for the school newspaper.

There were two rooms, the back office, which had a couch, a desk, and a long table probably meant for meetings, and the front workspace where the printing press rested in the center. By the front door, there was a small area in front of a counter with a number of chairs and a small table. It was common for newspaper print shops to be a place where people would gather for the latest news and gossip before it hit the presses. The *Boston Gazette* was no different. Only the *Gazette*, much like the Green Dragon, served as an unofficial meeting place for all things related to the rebellion.

JP recalled the night of the Boston Tea Party, when members of the Sons of Liberty met at the North Church and some came to the print shop to prepare their costumes.

"Everyone was dipping their fingers into the ink and wiping stripes onto their faces like the Mohawk Indians." He showed them the bottles of black and red ink. Alex could see the excitement in JP's eyes as he told the story of that night. "The Boston harbor was lit with a radiant moon and the excitement of two thousand townspeople cheering the Sons of Liberty as they crashed aboard the British ships loaded with tea." Alex and Hercules were riveted to his story. "We threw the King's tea into the harbor that night to the cries of *No taxation without representation!*"

THE DESTRUCTION OF TEA AT BOSTON HARBOR.

"Why'd you do it?" Hercules asked.

"The King had declared that we could only buy heavily taxed tea from the British East India Tea Company. This put a lot of the local merchants out of business and stressed our economy."

JP explained then pumped his fist in the air like he did on that fateful night.

"We threw the King's tea in the harbor to send him a message that he couldn't tax our tea or anything else, and we were not going to give up our liberties without a fight!"

That's the type of experience that Alex wanted. He came to America to be more than he could ever be back on the island of St. Croix. Now, here in Boston, he was finding an opportunity to be a part of something that could have lasting effects on history. Looking at the printing press in the middle of the work room, Alex thought of all the articles about key events that were likely printed on it; the protests against the Stamp Act and the Townsend Acts, the tragedy of the Boston Massacre, and the excitement of the Boston Tea Party. All those articles printed on this very press must have incited passion for the rebel movement underway in Boston. Alex was getting caught up in the revolutionary spirit that permeated this city. He saw endless possibilities for America, and he wanted to be a part of every moment.

JP finished showing them around the print shop and left them alone, locking the door on his way out. Alex and Hercules fought over who got the couch, that looked relatively comfortable, and who got the cot, which looked more like a medieval torture device than a bed. But, when Alex reminded Hercules about winning the bet when his chicken was the last chicken standing, Hercules was forced to relinquish the couch. As they turned out the lamps and settled under their blankets, Alex could hear Hercules still mumbling his disgust at losing the bet.

"Stupid chickens," he muttered as they fell asleep.

11
Running From Redcoats

Alex was sleeping surprisingly well for being in a strange place. Unfortunately, the same couldn't be said for Hercules, who was tossing and turning on the cot of terror all night. He was awake when he thought he heard a noise coming from the workshop in the front. He quietly walked over to Alex and lightly shook his shoulder.

"Hey Alex, wake up."

Alex woke up and focused his eyes to see Hercules hanging over him.

"What are you...?"

Hercules covered Alex's mouth with his hand. "Shhhh..., I think I hear someone in the front room."

Alex grabbed Hercules' hand away from his mouth and got up on his elbows, trying to listen for sounds. *Crash!* Went something onto the floor.

"There's definitely someone out there," Alex whispered. "Come on."

Alex walked slowly and softly to the door that was cracked open. Hercules was right behind him as they could hear things being flung around in the front room.

Alex got down on his knees and peered through the opening. Hercules bent over the top of him and looked as well. What they saw were three redcoat soldiers rummaging through the print shop. They were looking for something and tossing everything out of the way trying to find it. Alex and Hercules slowly backed away from the door.

"What do you think they're searching for?" Hercules whispered.

"I don't know, but we need to do something."

After all that Ben had done for them, Alex wasn't going to let these redcoats just break in and trash his business.

"Somehow we have to get them out of here," Alex said.

Taking a moment to think of their options, Alex came up with a plan.

"Put on your shoes, Herc; we're going to do some running."

Hercules wasn't sure he liked the sound of that, but he trusted that Alex knew what he was doing.

"We are not going to be able to get armed redcoats out of here by force. The only way they'll leave is if they chase us out of here."

Hercules thought for a moment. "Why would they do that?"

Alex smiled and put his hand on his buddy's shoulder. "You're going to have to make them mad."

Now that sounds more like it, Hercules thought.

Alex and Hercules crept back over to the cracked door. They could see the soldiers clearly in the moonlight coming through the print shop windows. Alex held up a paperweight he got from Ben's desk.

"When I throw this into the far corner, they'll turn towards the noise. When they do that, you bull rush them and knock them down. Then we'll both run out the front door, and hopefully they'll follow."

Hercules liked the plan but was worried about the getaway.

"What if the door is locked?"

Alex shook his head. "Why would they have locked the front door? They probably broke the lock to get in."

Hercules wasn't convinced. "Maybe they didn't come in the front door; they might have come in the back."

Good point, Alex thought. "Well, it's either the front door or the back; one of them is open. My guess is that these redcoats are too arrogant to sneak in the backdoor."

Hercules followed Alex's logic, but just in case, he was going to make sure he hit them hard enough to give Alex time to unlock the door if he had to.

Alex and Hercules got themselves ready for the attack. Alex was positioned at the opening in the doorway with Hercules directly to the side of him. Alex looked over to Hercules one last time and gave him a nod. Hercules nodded back that he was ready. Alex brought his right arm back, took aim, and flung the paperweight across the room, hitting the wall with a loud thud! The three soldiers, startled, turned quickly towards the noise.

Hercules pushed the door open and sprinted as fast as he could towards the soldiers. Coming in full force with his shoulder lowered, the powerful Hercules caught the first soldier right in the middle of his back, driving him forward into the other two soldiers directly in front of him. He hit them with such an impact the first soldier was actually airborne when he hit the other two. All three of the soldiers hit the ground hard, with Hercules's momentum causing him to land right on top of the pile.

Alex, running right behind Hercules, leapt over the pile of humanity. His toe caught someone's leg, tripping him slightly; he stumbled and rammed into the door. The door burst open with Alex falling into the street. He got up quickly and looked back for his friend. Hercules was picking himself off the pile. One of the soldiers made an attempt to grab Hercules's ankle but couldn't hang on. Hercules was up and running out the door.

Suddenly, Alex and Hercules found themselves running for their lives. Alex glanced back and saw that the soldiers were right behind them. As they were running, it occurred to Alex that they had no idea where they were going. Alex saw an alley between two houses and pointed towards it, so Hercules knew where to turn. They ran between the houses. The soldiers weren't gaining on them, but they weren't losing them either.

Running through the back yards, they ran around a storage shed and leapt over a short picket fence. Alex ran into a stable, Hercules followed; they zigzagged around the stalls, past the horses, and out the backside. Once through, they slowed and looked back to see if they lost them, but they had no such luck. Alex could hear Hercules starting to gasp for air and knew he wouldn't last in the chase much longer.

Around the corner, they ran into another backyard. Halfway across it, Alex came to a quick stop when he saw there was no way out. There were houses on both their right and their left, and in front of them was some sort of stable with a solid wall. There was nowhere to go. They couldn't turn around. They were trapped!

Hercules was bent over, with his hands on his knees, looking like he was ready to be sick. Alex scanned the area, looking for a way out. He saw a barrel right in front of the stable. Taking a running start, he was able to jump up on top of it and then hoist himself onto the roof of the stable. Hercules saw what Alex did but had a look of there was no way he could do the same. Just then the redcoats came running around the corner, giving Hercules no choice. He ran as fast as he could, jumped with all his might, and made it onto the barrel. From there, Alex helped pull him onto the rooftop.

They ran across the rooftop and jumped down about three feet onto another smaller stable rooftop. On this roof, there were crates stacked up. They went in and out the rows of crates like a maze. Coming out the other side, there was a long board that stretched about fifteen feet from their rooftop to the next. There was a pigpen with a giant sow asleep directly below the board. Alex went across first, walking quickly but carefully, so as not to fall. Hercules got on the board before Alex was off, and the board creaked and began to bend in the middle. Alex jumped off, and the board bounced back up, causing Hercules to nearly lose his balance, but he steadied himself and made it across.

Watching Hercules nearly fall gave Alex an idea. He quickly bent down and repositioned the board so that it was right at the edge, barely hanging on. They could hear the redcoats right behind them, so they ran across the rooftop and ducked behind a ledge as the redcoats came out of the maze of crates. Without hesitation, the first redcoat bounded onto the board, which bent in the middle and quickly gave way, sending the soldier and board crashing down ten feet onto the giant sow below. The second redcoat, who was right behind the first, couldn't stop his momentum and was falling into the pit as well when the third redcoat grabbed his arm and held him in mid-air above the pig pen. But the weight was too much to bear, and both went crashing into the mud. Having disappeared from sight, all Alex and Hercules heard was a terrible squealing noise from the sow and cursing from the redcoats. They could only imagine the sight it must have been.

At the end of the rooftop, they were able to jump down onto a shed and then back to the ground. Unsure if the redcoats were still able to follow them, Alex and Hercules took off running back down an alley and down the street a few blocks. When they thought it was safe, they slowed down to look back and make sure that they weren't still being followed. Completely out of breath, they ducked behind a building and collapsed to the ground. Doing everything he could to catch his breath, Hercules leaned over to Alex.

"Next time..." Hercules could barely talk. "Next time... we stay and fight.... Much... easier."

Hercules fell back exhausted. Alex was smiling, happy that they accomplished their mission of getting the redcoats out of Ben's print shop. The two of them lay there for nearly twenty minutes.

Slowly they made their way back to the Gazette, trying to be as inconspicuous as possible. When they got there, they hid across the street and waited to see if the redcoats were going to return. After nearly an hour, they were satisfied it was safe, and they returned to the back room of the Gazette. It was nearly impossible for Alex to sleep the rest of the night. All that excitement, and the possibility of the redcoats returning, kept Alex tossing and turning. For Hercules, on the other hand, all that exercise was just what he needed. Completely exhausted, Hercules was out cold. If Alex had any hope of getting anymore sleep, those hopes were quickly dashed by the loud and persistent snoring of his roommate. The only thing for Alex to do at this point was rest and wait for the morning.

12
Maggie and Alex

JP and Maggie arrived at the Gazette the next morning just as their father's partner, Mr. Gill, was getting ready to unlock the front door. When Mr. Gill looked down at the lock, he saw that it had been damaged. Pieces of wood around the lock were broken away as if someone tried to pry it open. When JP and Maggie walked up, they saw what Mr. Gill was looking at. Right away Maggie's thoughts went to Alex and Hercules. She squeezed past Mr. Gill, saw all the mess in the print shop, and ran towards the back room. When she opened the door, she saw Alex and Hercules. They were both awake and sitting on the couch. Alex's hair was sticking up every which way as evidence of a rough night. He saw the look of relief on Maggie's face when she came in.

"We're both alright," he said, a bit flattered that she was so worried.

"What on earth happened?" Maggie asked. "It looks like a tornado hit out there." Maggie pointed back towards the mess in the print shop.

Alex and Hercules got up and walked out of the back room and into the print shop to inspect the damage during the light of day.

Mr. Gill and JP were walking around in disbelief. Alex assumed that the man with JP was Ben's partner and went up to introduce himself.

"Mr. Gill, I'm Alex Hamilton, and this is my friend Hercules Mulligan." Alex held his hand out and shook Mr. Gill's hand. "As you probably can tell, the Gazette was broken into last night."

Alex could see that Mr. Gill wasn't too shocked by this information.

Alex recounted what happened. "There were three redcoat soldiers searching through everything. They didn't know we were sleeping in the back room, so we managed to surprise them and lure them out. They haven't been back since."

Mr. Gill started walking around checking out the damage. His main concern was the printing press in the middle of the room. He looked it up and down and found it to be untouched.

"Well, it would appear that I owe you a great deal of thanks. Besides the broken door and a mess on the floor, there doesn't appear to be any significant damage."

He looked at Alex and Hercules with appreciation.

"Thank you for getting the redcoats out of here when you did. I'm just glad you two weren't hurt during all of the mayhem."

Alex was glad to be of service. He looked over at Maggie, who was smiling now that everything was alright.

JP, who had worked many hours at his father's print shop, volunteered the services of everyone.

"Don't worry, Mr. Gill. With all of us working, we can have this place straightened up in time for today's edition."

JP was right; things looked a lot worse than they actually were. After about thirty minutes, you could barely tell that the place had been torn apart at all. Two other employees had shown up for work, and it was business as usual. The first order of business for Mr. Gill was to work on today's headline story,

Gazette Ransacked!

With the newspaper back up and running, Alex and Hercules could get back to finding the members of the Sons of Liberty that might be in danger. They decided to split up. Maggie would take Alex to see Abigail Adams about tonight's party, and JP would take Hercules to see Samuel Adams at the State House. Alex actually wished he was going to the State

House, where there would certainly be a lot more going on, but he couldn't complain; after all, he was getting to spend time with Maggie.

Before they left, JP and Hercules took a crack at trying to repair the front door lock, at least fixing it so that it would stay shut. Maggie looked at Alex and smiled big.

"Are you ready to meet Abigail?" Alex smiled back. "I'm looking forward to it."

He opened the front door for Maggie. "After you, my dear," he said like the perfect gentleman. Hercules scoffed at watching Alex act like a little puppy dog around Maggie. Alex knew Hercules would be giving him a look of disdain for his behavior, so he didn't bother to give him the satisfaction by looking back at Hercules as they left. Instead, Hercules looked over at JP, and both of them just shook their heads in disgust.

Alex and Maggie hadn't walked more than fifty feet from the Gazette when the mood went from flirtatious to defensive. Three soldiers walked in front of them and brought them to an abrupt halt. Alex didn't get a good look at the soldiers from last night, but he had to assume that these were the same three redcoats. One of them was wearing a sling to hold up his arm, and all three of their uniforms were soiled with mud. *Must have happened falling into the pig pen last night*, Alex thought.

"Can we help you?" Alex said, not knowing whether they recognized him.

"We'll be asking the questions," the leader of the three shot back.

One of the three soldiers circled around behind them, which made Alex and Maggie very uncomfortable. Maggie kept glancing back at the redcoat standing behind them, not sure what he was up to. Finally, after a bit of posturing and intimidation, the leader asked them, "Where were you last night?"

Alex didn't know what to say. If he said he was sleeping in the back room of the Gazette they would surely know it was him they were chasing last night. Not wanting to lie to the soldiers and yet not wanting to confess, Alex did the best he could.

"I was sleeping," Alex said innocently.

This wasn't a lie; it just wasn't the answer to the soldier's question. The soldier looked at him peculiarly, "Yes, but where were you sleeping?"

Alex did not want to be a witness against himself. He tried again to give a less than straight forward answer.

"I slept on the couch."

The soldier's face turned red with anger as he started losing patience with Alex. All three soldiers started moving in a little closer, in a threatening manner, when Maggie jumped into the conversation.

"He slept on our couch as a guest of our family."

This was also the truth. Maggie just hoped that they would assume the couch was at their home. The soldiers pondered whether these two were involved with what happened last night.

One soldier spoke up and said to the others, "There's no way that this little runt and his girlfriend knocked all three of us down. It wasn't them!" he insisted.

The lead soldier started thinking about the embarrassment of bringing these two in and having to admit that they got the best of them.

Conjuring up a laugh he said, "You're right. The guys that hit us were much bigger."

Alex was glad that Hercules wasn't with him, or they would have definitely figured it was them. Maggie had something different on her mind. She only heard one word when the soldier was talking....*girlfriend*. The soldiers took a step to the side.

"You two lovebirds can go on your way."

Alex, realizing they were doing their best to belittle him, gave the soldiers a look of disparagement as he passed by.

Once they were out of sight of the soldiers, Alex turned to Maggie.

"That was close." Alex started laughing. "Did you smell those guys? I wonder if they even washed up after falling in the pigpen?"

Alex saw that Maggie was acting weird.

"What's with you?" Alex asked.

"Oh, nothing." Maggie said with a strange look and a slight smile on her face.

Alex wasn't sure why she was suddenly acting so odd; he was just glad to be rid of those redcoats.

13
John Adams Makes a Case

Walking through the town of Boston on their way to see Abigail Adams, Maggie and Alex came across a gathering of people outside the Queen Street Courthouse. Some were holding signs, and others were shouting, "Hang them! Let them rot in jail!"

"What's this all about?" Alex asked.

"I'm not sure, but it's probably got something to do with a trial going on inside."

Maggie pushed her way through the crowd, with Alex trying to stay close. Once they got to the front, they saw a row of redcoats guarding the front gate entrance. Alex was disappointed they couldn't go in and watch the trial.

"It looks like this is as close as we'll get," Alex remarked.

Maggie wasn't about to give up so easily. "Follow me," she said grabbing Alex's hand and leading him back through the crowd. When they were clear of the crowd, Maggie led Alex along the wooden fence line and around the corner. There she found a missing board in the fence and managed to squeeze through it.

"Come on," Maggie said, "you want to see the trial, don't you?"

Alex looked both directions, to see if anyone was watching them, then turned sideways, and slipped through the opening. Maggie ran over to the building.

"Come over here to help me with this crate."

Alex and Maggie each grabbed a side of a crate and carried it over to the window. Maggie jumped up and peered into the window.

"It's the courtroom. Come up and look."

Alex jumped up beside Maggie, cupped his hands around his face to cut down the glare on the window, and looked inside.

The courtroom was filled to capacity. There was a three foot railing that divided the citizens from the judge and attorneys. It appeared to Alex that the man on trial was a redcoat soldier. *No wonder there is such an uproar out front*, he thought. The soldier's attorney was walking back and forth in front of the people who were casting their judgment with every word he said. It was obvious that this soldier hadn't an ally anywhere in the room, except his attorney. The attorney had an admirable quality that shown him to be a man of honor and integrity. Even though the entire room was against his client, he was trying in earnest to make a case for his client's innocence.

"Who is that attorney?" Alex asked.

Maggie looked at him and laughed at the question.

"That's John Adams."

Alex looked back into the courtroom, and then realized that it made perfect sense that the attorney defending the redcoat soldier was John Adams. At Kings College, Alex had studied what his professor called the most important case in modern law. It was the case in which John Adams represented the five soldiers accused of murder in the Boston Massacre. Adams took the case despite the entire town of Boston being against him, including his own cousin Samuel Adams. People thought it was professional suicide for Adams to defend the most hated men in Boston. But John Adams was a man who respected the law and believed that it was his duty to provide council to everyone regardless of how reprehensible the crime was or how guilty they seemed to be. Alex's professor said that by taking on that case and representing those hated soldiers, John Adams set precedence for the role of attorneys in our judicial system.

Even though John Adams managed to get his clients off on lesser charges, the Sons of Liberty still were able to use the event in their favor. Paul Revere engraved a picture of the Boston Massacre, which showed the redcoats mercilessly killing innocent patriots. Ben Edes ran a copy of the etching in the Boston Gazette, and it was picked up by other newspapers throughout the colonies. The image helped rally support for the plight of the people of Boston.

The Massacre perpetrated in King Street Boston on March 5.th 1770, in which Mess.rs Sam.l Gray, Sam.l Maverick, James Caldwell, Crispus Attucks & Patrick Carr were Killed, six others Wounded, two of them Mortally.

Maggie could see that Alex was inspired watching Adams work a courtroom.

"John Adams is one of the only attorneys who the British will allow to represent them in the colonies."

Alex was confused. "What do you mean 'in the colonies?'"

Maggie explained. "As part of the Coercive Acts, the British can send the trial back to England if they don't think they will get a fair trial here."

Alex couldn't believe it. How could they take a case away from the place where the crime was committed? How would there be any witnesses, evidence, or knowledge of the crime scene?

"It's like they are fixing the trials so that they will get the verdict to come out in their favor."

Maggie agreed. "Not only that but it allows for the British to operate above the law because if they get caught, their trials will be held back in the friendly confines of England."

Alex shook his head in disbelief.

"That's probably why those soldiers weren't too worried about breaking into the Gazette last night."

Alex looked back into the courtroom. Watching Adams continue to do what he believed was right, despite his own government

101

doing something in direct contrast to those ideals, made Alex respect Adams even more.

Maggie jumped down from the crate and waited for Alex, who was enjoying watching the proceedings.

"You know John Adams will be at the party tonight."

Alex jumped down.

"I'd love to talk to him and ask him about his cases." Alex said.

Maggie started to walk towards the opening in the fence. "Do you think he is one of the people in danger?" asked Maggie.

Alex thought about it for a second. "No, I don't." Alex followed Maggie squeezing between the boards. "I don't think the King is too worried about John Adams at this point."

Alex straightened his jacket after making it back through the fence. "I think that Samuel Adams is the target."

14
The State House

JP and Hercules arrived at the State House to see a whirlwind of activity. As part of the Coercive Acts, the British were taking control of the Massachusetts government. The first order of business was to replace Governor Thomas Hutchinson with British General Thomas Gage. Another way the British were going to regain control of the government was to move its capital away from all the trouble makers of Boston and into the more quiet town of Salem. When JP and Hercules arrived, every office was busy getting packed up for the move.

Walking through the front door of the State House, took a little while. Hercules held the door open for an elderly man carrying a big box. Right behind him were two people carrying a desk. JP quickly grabbed ahold of the desk, guiding it so that the desk could fit through. Hercules continued to hold the door for two ladies, who were walking back into the building, and a man walking out with a rolled up carpet on his shoulder. It was a continual parade of people back and forth through the front door. Hercules thought he would never get out of holding the door when he noticed a piece of triangular shaped wood by his feet. Hercules picked it off the ground and held it up to JP.

"I guess we're out of a job."

Hercules bent down and kicked the doorstop underneath the door holding it open.

Finally, getting into the huge foyer of the State House, Hercules was taken aback by the grand staircase in the center of the room. It was a beautiful winding staircase with mahogany handrails and white painted balusters. It went around and around up three stories and down one. Hercules had never seen anything like it. JP pointed up the stairs.

"Let's go to the second story. That's where all the Representatives have their offices."

Samuel Adams was elected to the Massachusetts Assembly nine years ago, largely because of the popularity he gained by writing articles in the *Boston Gazette* against the British Parliament. Ever since that time, he had been the colonies' leading voice in favor of the Massachusetts Assembly making decisions in their own colony instead of the British Parliament using the colony as a source of revenue for the King.

Now, things had gotten even worse under the Coercive Acts. The Assembly was being forced by the British Parliament to move out of Boston. As JP climbed the winding stairs, he was a bit concerned that Samuel Adams might not be too happy today. He could hear Samuel making some sort of snide comment about moving to Salem and the British conducting another witch hunt.

The upstairs hallways were full of items ready to be carried downstairs and then transported to Salem. Hercules followed JP to the offices of Samuel Adams. When they walked inside, they saw something that they simply weren't expecting to see. Wall to wall redcoats were packing all of Samuel Adams belongings into big trunks.

"This can't be good," Hercules said as they looked around the room for Samuel Adams.

JP walked up to one of the soldiers. "Excuse me. Do you know where Mr. Adams is?"

The soldier looked over the two civilians from head to toe. "Who wants to know?" The soldier barked at them.

JP, who was a pretty quick thinker, responded, "We're Mr. Adams' messengers checking in for work."

It was common for Representatives to have young people be messengers, or pages, who would run errands for them.

"Well, there's no work for you today. Your boss got hauled off in chains about an hour ago."

JP couldn't believe it. Samuel Adams had a fiery personality and probably had a lot of difficulty accepting today's move, but to be hauled off in chains seemed a bit extreme.

"What happened?" Hercules asked.

"From what I saw, Mr. Adams refused to move his office, so the captain ordered us to start moving Mr. Adams items out for him. Mr. Adams protested and went marching into the Judge's office. A few minutes later, he was being ushered out of the building with his hands chained behind his back."

JP thanked the soldier for the information and headed out the door.

When they got out of the office, JP and Hercules looked out over the grand staircase, stopped, and wondered what to do next. As they watched all the people walking up on the left side and down on the right, someone caught JP's eye. JP leaned way over the rail to get a better look. Hercules quickly grabbed onto the back of JP's shirt tail.

"Careful there, buddy," Hercules said, pulling JP backward away from the railing. "Who did you see?"

Before he answered, JP took off down the stairs. Hercules followed him, weaving in and out of all the people. When they got down to the lobby, JP yelled to a man who was just heading out the door.

"Mr. Hancock!"

JP followed him out the door and caught up to him right outside the building.

John Hancock was a friend of his father and had been over to his house on many occasions. He looked positively beside himself when JP walked up to him.

"Mr. Hancock, I was wondering if you might have a moment."

John Hancock's mind was elsewhere when JP came up to him.

"Oh, JP, well, yes, of course, how can I help you?"

Just then Hercules caught up to them.

"This is my friend Hercules Mulligan from New York. Hercules, this is John Hancock."

Hercules held his hand out.

"It's a pleasure to meet you, sir."

Mr. Hancock shook Hercules's hand.

"Welcome to Boston, the town that is covered in red and now being turned upside down."

Mr. Hancock was obviously upset about something. Hercules, not knowing quite what to say in return, just smiled. Noticing that his greeting to Hercules was a bit unorthodox, John tried again.

"I'm sorry, fellows; I am just a bit bent out of shape right now after talking to one of our dirty judges about a friend of mine."

Putting recent events together, JP asked, "By chance, would that friend be Samuel Adams?"

John Hancock shook his head. "Yes, how did you know?"

"We were looking for Mr. Adams when the redcoats told us he was taken away in irons."

Mr. Hancock shook his head in agreement of the story and put his arm around JP, leading him away from the State House.

"Come over here, away from the sharp ears of the redcoats."

Once away from the shadow of the State House, Mr. Hancock told them about his visit to the judge.

"Apparently, Sam went into the judge's office accusing the redcoats of stealing his belongings. The judge, in turn, ordered the soldiers to take him away and put him in the pillory."

Mr. Hancock looked around to see if anyone was eavesdropping on their conversation.

"I know this judge, and he's no friend of the Sons of Liberty. I'm sure he wanted to make an example of Sam by embarrassing him."

This didn't seem right to Hercules, "Can a judge just sentence a man like that?"

"Not without a trial by a jury of his peers he can't. It seems like the British may have their own set of laws." Hancock said, his face getting flush just thinking about it. "Anyway, like I said, I know this judge, and I know that he's on the take." Hancock looked over his shoulder one more time. "So, I paid the guy off to get Sam out."

Hercules couldn't believe that the justice system was operating like this.

"Now, normally I would have never done such a thing, but we can't afford to have a man as important to the cause as Sam locked up." Clenching his teeth in frustration, Hancock justified his actions. "Desperate times call for desperate measures."

JP remembered his own feelings of doubt when he participated in the unloading of tea into Boston Harbor.

"Getting our freedoms back is what is most important to all of us right now," JP told Mr. Hancock, trying to offer his support. "If we have any chance at freedom, we need men like you and Samuel Adams leading the way."

Mr. Hancock looked JP in the eyes and put his hand on his shoulder.

"You've grown to be a good man, JP, just like your father."

JP felt honored to be compared to his greatly admired father.

"Come with me, gentlemen." John Hancock said, motioning his hand for them to join him. "Let's go get our feisty friend out of the pillory."

JP, Hercules, and John Hancock walked purposefully down the street. The nearest pillory was located in the town square in front of Faneuil Hall. JP had seen people stuck in the pillory before, but he couldn't imagine a man like Samuel Adams with his hands and head locked in the wooden stockade.

15
Stuck in a Pillory

It was the middle of the day, and the sun was bearing down on the town of Boston. While walking to the pillory, JP thought about the irony of Samuel Adams being stuck in a pillory in front of Faneuil Hall. Faneuil Hall was the largest auditorium in Boston and the preferred spot for town meetings. Members of the Sons of Liberty often spoke at these meetings and none more passionately than Samuel Adams. It became difficult to think of Faneuil Hall without thinking of Samuel Adams. After JP heard John Hancock's description of this vindictive judge, it was no wonder that he chose the site of Samuel Adams' greatest triumphs as the site for his greatest humiliation. JP could hardly stand the thought.

When they entered the square, John Hancock kept walking straight towards his friend stuck in the pillory. JP and Hercules, on the other hand, had to pause at the sight before them. The square was always a busy place, and today was no exception. There were people moving about, farmers selling produce out of their wagons, and children playing hopscotch.

Yet there was one difference. Today, everyone in the square knew the man that was in the pillory. The Tories in the square were enjoying every minute.

"You had this coming, Adams!" they yelled while shaking their fists in the air. At the same time, Adams' friends did their best to defend the town's leading patriot, and then there was Samuel Adams, a prisoner serving a cruel and unusual punishment. He was slumped over with his head and his hands poking out the front of the pillory. It looked to be very uncomfortable to Hercules and, more than that, very embarrassing. There were smashed fruit and vegetables on and under the pillory, clinging to Samuel's forehead, and even in his hair. Yet, through it all, Samuel Adams wasn't a defeated man. He was yelling at everyone who yelled at him and handling the situation the best he could.

As Hercules looked out over the scene, he noticed a couple of particularly obnoxious boys right in front of them. One of the boys reached into a sack he was carrying and pulled out a rotten tomato. He must have brought it from home for the sole purpose of firing it at whatever poor soul was in the pillory.

The boy brought his arm back and prepared to throw. Just as he was ready to let it fly, the boy's arm came to a sudden stop. Still holding the tomato in his hand, a stocky, red headed man had a hold of his wrist.

"Don't you know who that is in the pillory?" asked Hercules.

The boy answered him with a sneer on his face. "No, who cares?"

Not liking the boy's disrespectful attitude, Hercules put his other hand over the boy's hand, holding the tomato, and slowly began to squeeze.

"I care," said Hercules, as tomato juice began running down the boy's arm followed by tomato mush. JP started walking away.

"Come on, Hercules, stop goofing off, and let's go help Sam."

Hercules let go of the boy, who just stared at his hand full of tomato mush. His friend started laughing at his misfortune, which resulted in the tomato boy chasing his friend around the square with his gross hand.

JP and Hercules walked over to the pillory where John Hancock was already negotiating Samuel Adams' release. There was a redcoat assigned to watch over the prisoner while he was in the pillory. Mr. Hancock pulled out a folded sheet of paper from his coat pocket and handed it to the soldier. It was an order from the judge to free Samuel Adams from the pillory. The soldier looked it over, then somewhat disappointedly said, "Everything seems to be in order," and he put the paper in his own jacket pocket.

When his friend John Hancock showed up for his rescue, Sam's ranting changed from anger to sarcasm.

"I sure am glad to see you, John. I was getting worried that these poor boys might wear their arms out throwing so much fruit at me."

Hancock laughed and added, "It's hard to blame them when they have the opportunity to throw at a target as big as your head."

The redcoat was fumbling to undo the lock.

"Just my luck today," remarked Sam, "I get put into a stockade with a faulty lock made in England instead of a quality lock made here."

"Do they even make locks here, Sam?" Hancock asked.

"I don't know, but if they did, THEY WOULD DARN WELL OPEN!" Sam said, raising his voice in frustration.

The soldier stopped trying to open it, and he thought for a moment. Reaching into his other pocket, he pulled out a different key. John Hancock saw the soldier make the switch but fortunately Sam did not. The soldier put the new key in the lock, and it opened right up.

After the soldier removed the lock, Hancock lifted the top portion of the pillory up, allowing his friend to gain his freedom. Sam stood up straight, stretched his back out, rolled his neck a few times, and moved his arms about.

With one deep breath and a thankful handshake to John Hancock, Samuel Adams was ready to fight another day.

"I assume that you had to use your powers of persuasion with the judge to get me out of there."

John Hancock raised his eyebrows. "Unfortunately the scoundrel required an excessive amount of persuasion before he saw things my way."

Sam slapped John on the back a few times.

"You're a great friend, and you can count on me to be there for you if the circumstances are ever reversed."

"No offense," John responded, "I prefer my role over yours just fine."

As they walked out of the square, JP introduced Hercules to Samuel Adams.

"Hercules is a tailor in New York and overheard a conversation that I think is important for both of you to hear."

Hercules was a bit intimidated without having Alex by his side.

"Well, what did you hear that brings you all the way from New York?" asked Sam Adams.

Hercules hesitated once again. Then he remembered that he still had his drawing of the lion on top of the crosses Ben Edes identified. He searched in his pockets and pulled out the crumpled paper with his sketch on it. Handing it to Samuel Adams, he said, "There were two men who we think are trying to bring harm to the leaders of the Sons of Liberty. They had invitations to a party where they are planning to attack."

Hercules pointed to his paper, "I saw that design on the top of the invitations."

Sam Adams took one quick look at the sketch and recognized it immediately. He showed it to John Hancock.

"Look familiar?"

John looked at it a bit, and then it hit him.

"Abigail's party!"

Samuel Adams put his arm around Hercules' shoulder and started walking with him.

"I'm going to need to know exactly what these men said."

Hercules was getting worried that he might say something wrong and wished that Alex was there to talk for him.

"Mr. Adams, I'll tell you all I know, but you really should talk with my friend Alexander Hamilton. He'll be able to give you more information."

"Well, we can talk to Alexander later," Samuel Adams assured Hercules, "Why don't you tell me all that you can now."

John could see that Hercules was a little rattled.

"You're a brave man, Hercules, and I'm glad the Sons of Liberty have you on our side."

Hercules felt good about being able to help out and tried his best to tell Samuel Adams everything he could remember about the two strangers and what they said.

16
Amazing Abigail

Abigail Adams was busy getting ready for tonight's party. She was enjoying the use of John Hancock's beautiful mansion. The Adams family had moved out of town a few years ago when things started to get too dangerous in Boston. Abigail appreciated the quiet setting of a village called Braintree and the peace of mind that her family was safe. Yet, for her husband, John, the ten mile ride by horse was less than convenient. As an attorney, John's livelihood was in Boston, so the long trip couldn't be avoided.

John Adams had managed, for the most part, to stay out of the political protests that permeated the Boston community. Although he didn't agree with the actions of the British Parliament, he was not comfortable with the aggressive nature of the protests and wished for a more diplomatic approach. However, that was all changing as the intrusions of the British government became more vindictive and less than cordial. John Adams slowly came to believe that a more forceful stance must be taken in order to counter the British tactics of punishment. It was time for John to take on a more active role in the Sons of Liberty, like his cousin Samuel. Hosting a party tonight and inviting the Sons of Liberty was a step in that direction.

Abigail had always been supportive of her husband's endeavors and agreed to organize the party for him. There probably wasn't a man in all of Massachusetts who benefitted from his wife more than John Adams. Abigail was a highly intelligent woman who provided John with a perspective that enabled him to accomplish matters that he simply wouldn't be able to accomplish without her. Anyone who knew the Adams's knew that Abigail was a great source of strength for John. She had the ability to engage the sharpest minds of Boston in thoughtful conversation on topics of politics and government, while remaining well-grounded in taking care of the homestead and her four children. John often came to Abigail seeking her opinion on a particular dilemma he was having. She served as his advisor and, in many ways, his conscience.

When Alex and Maggie arrived at the Hancock mansion, they found Abigail at the front door directing John Hancock's staff in their preparation for tonight's party. Abigail was always fond of Maggie, who would often help her look after the children. When she saw

Maggie and Alex walk up the path towards the home, a look of delight came over her.

"Maggie Edes, just the person I was hoping to see."

Abigail gave her a big hug and a kiss on the cheek as if she were her own daughter.

"Mrs. Adams, this is my friend, Alexander Hamilton, from New York."

Alex took his hat off and bowed his head slightly.

"It's a pleasure to meet you, Mrs. Adams."

Abigail welcomed Alex and gave Maggie a quick look of approval. Maggie saw the look but tried not to acknowledge it in case Alex was watching.

"I'm glad you two are here. There is still so much work left to do before the party."

Abigail motioned for them to come in and follow her. As they walked into the foyer, Alex watched as Maggie's eyes sparkled when she looked up at the magnificent crystal chandelier that was dangling high overhead.

"Mr. Hancock had the chandelier imported from Murano, Italy," Maggie told Alex as they passed under the centerpiece of the two story foyer.

All Alex could think about was how difficult it would be to light the candles on something that high, but then he saw the chain used to lower it for lighting. The foyer had two staircases, one curving from the left and the other from the right, which met at the top. There were two sets of glass French doors on each side of the foyer. One lead to a study that was elegantly furnished and had massive bookcases that spanned from floor to ceiling. The other set of doors lead to a parlor that had been cleared out of all furnishings, leaving it with an expansive parquet dance floor.

When Maggie entered the parlor, she couldn't help but spread her arms out and twirl around as if she were dancing at the ball. Abigail smiled at Maggie's excitement but called out to her, "Come now, there is plenty of work to be done."

Before they knew it, Alex and Maggie were in the kitchen helping fold cocktail napkins. Maggie told Abigail they saw Mr. Adams defending the soldier down at the courthouse. Abigail was very proud of John holding strong to his beliefs.

"John has a great deal of respect for the rights of all men to be equal. He'll defend that soldier with every bit as much vigor as he would his best friend."

Alex could see the same passion that John Adams had in the courtroom in Abigail Adams when she spoke about equality.

"Both John and I hope that the principles of men like John Locke and Montesquieu can one day be the principles that rule this land."

What John and Abigail were most concerned about in the colonies was that the King and Parliament were focused too much on the laws of England and were losing sight of the laws of nature.

"John Locke thought that all men were created equal and should be allowed to enjoy the pleasures of life, liberty, and property." Abigail preached to Alex and Maggie.

Her face was full of the passion and conviction of those ideals.

"They may not find those words in the Magna Carta, the English Bill of Rights, or any other document, but that doesn't mean that the people don't have those rights."

Alex was mesmerized listening to Abigail. If she took up arms and lead them into battle, Alex would have no hesitation in following her.

"These rights are inalienable," Abigail looked directly into the eyes of her young audience, "they cannot be taken from us no matter what government may or may not write with quill and paper."

Alex was stunned by how easily these words flowed from Abigail's lips. She spoke of the laws of man as if they were self-evident and that she was only stating what was already realized in nature. Abigail continued to move about the kitchen, getting ready for the party as she spoke, never once breaking stride.

While Abigail and Maggie were tending to some glassware, Alex noticed that a squirrel had jumped up onto the windowsill. The window was open, and there was a large jar of tea brewing in the sunlight. The squirrel was nosing around the tea and up on his hind legs. Alex went over to the window and scared the squirrel off of the windowsill and onto the ground.

"What happened?" asked Abigail.

"There was a squirrel nosing around the tea. Do you want me to throw it out?"

Abigail wasn't one to waste anything. "Did you see it drinking from the jar?"

Alex thought for a second. "I didn't see its head in the jar, but it may have when I wasn't looking."

"Well, if you didn't see it take a drink, we'll assume that it's good." Abigail said. "That isn't any ordinary tea."

Alex looked a little closer.

The tea was about the same color as regular tea, but this jar had pine needles in it.

Abigail explained, "The Daughters of Liberty have tried to help the cause by making our own products to take the place of the ones we are boycotting. We make our own clothes, soap, candles, and even tea."

Alex looked at the jar of pine needles and was still wondering why they were in the tea.

Maggie chimed in. "We don't have any tea leaves, so we use the pine needles instead."

"How's it taste?" asked Alex.

Abigail and Maggie both had a look on their face like they just sucked on a lemon.

"Let's just say that the symbolism is what is most important. In fact, this batch was sent here, probably by one of the Daughters of Liberty, to be used in a toast tonight."

Alex had nearly forgotten why he came here in the first place.

"That reminds me, Mrs. Adams; I wanted to speak to you about your guests at the party tonight."

Abigail figured there was a reason that Alex had come all the way from New York. She didn't think it was just to frighten squirrels away from her pine needle tea. Alex told Abigail the story of how Hercules overheard the two strangers plotting some sort of attack on, he presumed, the Sons of Liberty. He also told her about the invitations that they were holding to tonight's party.

"Do you have a guest list of all those who will be attending?" asked Alex.

Abigail didn't see how these strangers could obtain an invitation, never the less two.

"I have a list, but it's back at my house."

Alex was hopeful that they could figure out who the strangers were by looking at the guest list.

"Did everybody RSVP?"

Abigail thought about the confirmations and said, "Everyone but Benedict Arnold up in Connecticut, but I didn't expect him to come all the way down here for a party. He doesn't seem that committed to the cause. The invitation was just a courtesy."

Alex wasn't sure how they could determine who these men were. Maggie had an idea.

"We could put Hercules at the front door to welcome the guests. He would be able to recognize the two men."

Knowing Hercules, Alex wasn't so sure that would be a good idea.

"I'd be worried that the strangers might identify Hercules before he could identify them, and that may put him in danger."

Alex thought a little more about figuring out who these guys were.

"How did you print all the invitations, Mrs. Adams?"

Alex knew what Abigail was going to say but wanted to confirm it.

"Why, I had Ben Edes print them, of course."

Alex thought if the strangers were not using one of Ben's printed invitations, which would all be identical, then they must have made a hand copied version for themselves.

"We could put a doorman at the front door to collect invitations. He would be able to look at the crest and spot if any of the invitations looked different from the ones that Mr. Edes made."

It sounded like a good plan.

"But, what do we do when we know who it is?" asked Maggie.

Alex thought about it for a moment and said, "We'll have an entire mansion full of members of the Sons of Liberty. We'll let them know who the strangers are, and I'm sure they'll take care of the threat in no uncertain terms."

Abigail decided she would keep a watch out for the strangers as well. *Nobody is going to ruin an Adams party*, she thought.

17
Furniture Metaphors

Once everything was done in the kitchen that Abigail wanted done, she asked Alex and Maggie to help her in the study. The room had a very warm feel to it. In the back of the room was the massive bookshelf that covered nearly the entire wall. Directly opposite the bookshelf were six windows that were four feet wide by ten feet tall. They were surrounded by long, flowing garnet colored drapes held open with golden ropes. The other two walls were covered with mahogany paneling, which gave the room its warmth and richness. Scattered amongst the paneling were pieces of art, mostly portraits by popular British artists like William Hogarth and Joshua Reynolds. It was a room that welcomed you in and then begged you to stay. Alex could see why Maggie was so excited about having the party here.

When Abigail entered the room, she began assessing the furniture to determine where everything should go. There were thirteen pieces of furniture, which included a large wooden desk, three couches, two end tables, a coffee table, and six chairs of various shapes and sizes. Abigail wanted to allow for people to be seated near each other for conversation, yet she also wanted to open up the room so that people could stand and circulate.

Alex, always wanting to help out and solve a problem, asked, "Will everyone already know each other?"

Abigail was more than used to a man trying to take control of a situation, having lived with John for so many years.

"Everyone is from Massachusetts and knows each other quite well."

Alex could tell by the way she said *Massachusetts,* that Abigail had a great deal of pride in her colony.

"Have you lived your whole life in Massachusetts?" Alex asked to make conversation.

"I have, and I wouldn't think of living anywhere else."

Abigail picked up a small chair and moved it towards one of the corners.

"You'll find, Mr. Hamilton, that most people are very loyal to their colonies. Many of them affectionately refer to their home colony as their country. For John and me, our loyalties lie with Massachusetts more than with England."

Abigail seemed to have figured out how she wanted to set up the room.

"Come here, you two."

Abigail's eyes were looking at each piece of furniture and mentally placing them in different areas of the room.

"What we're going to do is divide the room into three separate sitting areas."

She pointed around the room as she spoke.

"Alex, you can look at these thirteen pieces of furniture as the thirteen British colonies. We're going to divide them into the New England colonies, the middle colonies, and the southern colonies."

Alex looked around the room at the furniture and started seeing the colonies.

"Okay, I get it."

He walked over to some of the older chairs with traditional styling and elegant upholstery.

"These small chairs can be used for the New England colonies."

"Good," said Abigail. "Let's move them over to this part of the room."

She moved them toward the North wall by the bookshelves. Maggie was getting the hang of it now and walked over by one of the couches.

"These couches are larger and meant for relaxation, so they could be the southern colonies."

"That's right, Maggie" Abigail remarked, satisfied that her metaphor was working out.

"Let's move those two couches and an end table over towards the window, so they will catch the sunlight."

Alex grabbed one end of the couch and Maggie the other, and they moved it towards the windows. Abigail walked over towards the desk.

"Let's move the remaining furniture over in this direction under the portraits. We can have the last couch and two chairs along with the coffee table represent our middle colonies"

After everything was moved into position, Abigail surveyed the room again and liked what she saw. She walked over to one of the chairs by the bookshelf. Standing behind the chair she said, "This is my favorite chair. It's probably the oldest chair in the room, but with age comes character."

Abigail walked around to the front of the chair. "I like the blue velvet upholstery. It reminds me of the ocean." Abigail sat down and settled back into the chair. "It's probably not right for everyone, but for me, it feels the most comfortable."

Abigail looked directly at Alex as if she were going to tell him something important. "You know, if I were the only one in this room, I would sit in this chair and be most content, but tonight, with all these people here, it's important that everyone can use any of the chairs as if they were all their own."

Alex stopped and thought for a moment. He understood what Abigail was saying and added his own analysis. "It wouldn't work if everybody insisted on sitting in just their favorite chair; it only works if we think of all the furniture as part of a larger seating area."

Maggie was getting thoroughly confused. "Are we still talking about furniture, or are we talking about the colonies?"

Alex laughed at their coded language.

"Mrs. Adams was pointing out that Massachusetts could not be the only colony standing up for its rights. If we are going to be successful in our fight with the British, we will have to unite as one. The Romans were fond of saying *e pluribus Unum*, which is Latin for *out of many one.*"

Abigail got up from her seat. She walked a little around the room assessing the furniture.

"But what we have to always remember is that the colonies, or states, still must maintain an important role in government. What is good for one state might not work for the next. There are certain things that need to be dealt with by the people of each state. A government that understands that balance, between the interests of the country with the interests of its states, is a government that will be successful."

It was getting late, and Alex and Maggie still had to meet back up with Hercules at the Edes house to compare notes on the day. Abigail walked over to a hall closet and pulled out some scarlet clothes.

"Before you go, why don't you take these."

Abigail handed Maggie a fancy full- length apron with ruffles and handed Alex a matching scarlet vest.

"I figured you two could pose as hired help for the party tonight."

Alex thought that was a good idea, but he couldn't help but wonder if Abigail was a little short on help and just roped them in.

"Would you have another vest for my friend Hercules?"

Abigail headed back to the closet.

"Why, of course. Is he about the same size?"

Alex looked at his own vest, which looked a little small.

"You better make it a bigger one."

Abigail handed the second vest to Alex and walked them back through the foyer and to the front door.

"Let's hope that we're able to identify those strangers tonight. I'm sure if you point them out to Sam, he'll take care of them before they get a chance to take care of him."

That's the idea, thought Alex, as he waved goodbye.

18
A Chicken Conspiracy

When Alex and Maggie arrived back at the Edes residence, they found Hercules in the backyard amongst the chickens again. He was at the far end of the yard and working on something up against the fence. As Alex and Maggie moved closer, they could see that he was using twine to attach a scarecrow to the fence. The scarecrow was wearing a straw hat on top of a burlap sack head full of acorns, and on his body was an old tweed shirt.

Alex had to smile when he thought about all the times Hercules was doing something a little offbeat. Alex liked that about him. Hercules always kept him on his toes, never knowing what he'd do next.

"Did you find yourself a new best friend?" Alex laughed.

After securing the scarecrow, Hercules turned around, "Well, if I had, at least he wouldn't conspire against me with chickens."

They all started laughing at the thought of the chicken that wouldn't fall.

"You're still mad about that, aren't you?"

Hercules smiled, but Alex could see he was a little flustered. "Well, maybe a little." Hercules shook his head to clear his thoughts.

"Were you able to find Samuel Adams or John Hancock today?" asked Alex.

"Yeah, I found both of them. They're pretty good guys. But I'll tell you one thing; Sam Adams is definitely one of the people the two strangers are targeting."

Alex figured as much, after seeing him the night before presiding over the crowd. "What about John Hancock?"

Hercules was continuing to straighten the hat on the scarecrow's head. "He might be a target as well, mostly because he's pretty good friends with Sam Adams, and he has a lot of money to put to the fight."

After seeing Hancock's incredible mansion today, Alex could see how the British might be leery of people with money helping the cause of the patriots. Hercules took a few steps back and admired his scarecrow.

Alex had to ask, "So, what's the scarecrow for?"

Hercules looked over towards a stack of hay bales off to the side. "Come on over here. I want to show you something."

Alex and Maggie followed Hercules through a scattering of chickens and over to the hay bales. On top of the bales were two identical pistols.

"Look at these."

Hercules handed one to Alex. Alex had seen dueling pistols displayed before, but had never actually held one. Holding it in both hands, the first thing he noticed was how it was balanced differently than other pistols he had shot. It had a walnut handle with an engraving of a fancy "**B.E.**" on the side. After letting Alex examine it for a while, Hercules wanted to tell him about them. "These are genuine smooth bore, single shot, flintlock dueling pistols. JP showed them to me."

Maggie recognized them and said, "My father got them as a gift from a gunsmith who owed him money. He's not planning on having a duel or anything."

Maggie thought the whole idea of dueling was a barbaric practice by stubborn men with too much pride for their own good. Hercules and Alex were more caught up in the excitement of the finely crafted pistols.

"JP said that we could fire them one time." Hercules told Alex, grinning ear to ear.

"You want to have a duel?" Alex asked, not sure what kind of crazy ideas Hercules had in his head.

"No, of course not, we can stand side by side, pace off like a real duel, but in the same direction, and then turn and fire at the scarecrow. First one to hit it wins."

Alex was impressed by the amount of planning Hercules had done for this.

"This is still trying to get even after the whole chicken thing, isn't it?"

Alex accused Hercules, who shrugged his shoulders and said, "Well, what do you say? Are you up for the challenge?"

Alex looked down at the scarecrow and then at the pistol in his hand; a smile came over his face. "I accept your challenge."

Hercules knew he would. "Great, now we just have to figure out how to load these things."

Maggie rolled her eyes and reached for the pistols. "Give them to me. I'll take care of that."

Alex and Hercules just looked at each other and watched in amazement as Maggie went about putting the powder in, packing it down, and loading the ammunition. The sight brought Alex back to the other day when they mistook Maggie for a boy with her hair up under her hat and wearing a big coat. *That's one incredible girl*, Alex thought as he watched her handle the pistols.

With their pistols cocked and loaded, Alex and Hercules stood shoulder to shoulder about twenty feet in front of the scarecrow. They received their instructions from Maggie, who was serving as the official judge.

"Remember, the first one to hit the scarecrow after I yell *fire* is the champion."

Maggie walked off to the side and took her position. Alex and Hercules turned their backs toward the scarecrow and awaited their instructions. Alex couldn't help but to rib Hercules one more time.

"Your strength is going to be no match for my quickness, big guy."

Hercules smiled. "I'm deceptively fast when I have to be, like a rattlesnake that lulls you to sleep, then, Bam!"

Alex laughed, not being able to picture his friend as a rattlesnake.

Maggie brought the combatants to attention.

"Duelist, take you marks... and march... one ...two...three..."

Alex and Hercules paced side by side with their pistols in front of them. Chickens were scurrying to get out of the way as they marched forward. Maggie continued the count. "Seven...eight...nine...ten."

Alex's heart was beating hard as they came to a halt. Everything seemed deadly silent as they stood there waiting their next command. Alex could hear Hercules breathing incredibly loud next to him.

Then, suddenly, Maggie called, "Turn," as they both pivoted towards the scarecrow, Maggie yelled at the top of her lungs, "FIRE!"

She yelled so loud it sent the chickens flying up in front of them. Hercules, shocked from the chickens and the yelling, whirled around and sent off an erratic shot that went whistling skyward nowhere near the scarecrow.

Immediately he looked over at Alex, who had held his fire. Alex slowly raised his pistol.

"No fair!" Hercules protested.

"Did you see those chickens get in the way?"

Alex blocked Hercules out of his mind and took careful aim at the scarecrow.

"Those chickens are sabotaging me!" Hercules cried out.

Alex, under complete control, locked in on his target and pulled the trigger, sending a plume of smoke from the gun and a near simultaneous explosion of acorns in the air as the scarecrow's head exploded upon impact.

Maggie jumped up, yelled, and clapped. This time she ran over to Alex with her arms outstretched.

"My hero!" she said, giving Alex a big hug.

Once again Hercules was left with his shoulders slouched down and his head fallen to the side like a rag doll. In disbelief, his frustration boiled over, and he focused on his real enemies.

"You think I don't know what you're up to!"

Hercules bent down and tried to stare a chicken in the face.

"You think you can make a fool out of me don't you!"

He was yelling like a man who had lost his mind. Alex and Maggie couldn't stop laughing. Hercules pointed his gun at the nearest chicken and pulled the trigger, which harmlessly went *click*.

He chased another chicken and fired at it also, *click*.

Around and around Hercules ran after the chickens, *click, click, click*, until he was too tired to run anymore. He fell to his knees and lay down on his back.

"I surrender," Hercules said, out of breath and accepting defeat.

As he lay there looking like da Vinci's Vitruvian Man spread out on the ground, a chicken came pecking around him, moved between his chest and arm, and settled itself down right in his armpit. Hercules slowly turned his head and saw the chicken lying in his armpit, mocking his very existence. He turned his head back towards the sky, let out a deep sigh, and mumbled the words, "stupid chickens."

19
Boston's Finest

Abigail was glad to see Alex, Hercules, and Maggie arrive at the mansion. They were decked out in their scarlet uniforms and had arrived early as she had asked.

"Don't you gentlemen look handsome."

Abigail complimented Alex and Hercules as they entered the foyer, "Maggie, you are absolutely breath-taking. I'm afraid the ladies at the party are going to be a bit jealous when my waitress grabs all the attention."

Abigail told Maggie to wear a dress under her scarlet apron. She decided to go all out and wear her favorite dress; after all, the party was at the Hancock mansion. She was probably over dressed for serving hors d'oeuvres, but she couldn't pass up the opportunity to dress up for a big party. From the look on Alex's face when he saw her, Maggie knew she made the right decision.

At the Mansion, John Hancock's regular staff of maids and butlers were wearing the same scarlet clothes as the three of them. When Alex saw the doorman, he introduced himself and explained to him that he was to look for two men with invitations that were slightly different from the rest. Hercules also did his best to give the doorman a good description of what the two strangers looked like.

Once inside, the three of them, and Abigail, went over the plan for the night. Alex and Maggie would circulate the party, serving drinks and hors d'oeuvres, while Hercules worked behind the bar in the back room. Everyone was to be on the lookout for anything out of the ordinary.

"How do you think those two strangers are going to attack tonight?" asked Hercules, who envisioned a major gun battle unfolding.

"Maybe we should be looking for pistols under their jackets or maybe even a knife."

Alex wasn't so sure if it would be that straight forward.

"They could try to threaten Sam Adams or blackmail John Hancock. They could frame them and then have them arrested on some made up charge."

Alex got a real serious look on his face. "We have to be ready for anything. People's lives could be in danger tonight."

They all agreed to be vigilant and pay attention to everything that was happening. If they saw something, they would report it to Ben or Samuel, and they could decide what to do about it.

Everything was set when the guests began to arrive. There were three musicians playing music in the Foyer as people came through the front door. Abigail instructed them to remain in the foyer until all the guests arrived and then move into the ballroom for the remainder of the evening. Alex and Maggie were set up to serve drinks and hors d'oeuvres in the study, while Hercules was working the bar, which was located just behind the study. When John Hancock had the mansion built, he had a separate smaller room made in the back with a bar in it to entertain small groups of friends from time to time. By putting Hercules behind the bar and out of sight, it lessoned the chances that the strangers would recognize him and blow their cover.

As the guests arrived, the doorman opened the door for them taking their invitations, and one of the butlers took their hats and jackets to a back closet. Abigail and John Adams stationed themselves in the foyer so that they could see when guests arrived and welcomed them to the party. Eventually, the guests would make it into the study.

As they walked in, Maggie leaned over to Alex and told him who each of them were. Since most of them were acquaintances of her father, she recognized just about everyone.

"There's George Hewes and his wife Sally, Thomas Melville and his fiancé, I'm not sure what her name is, but they are to be married in August."

An elderly man walked in. "That's James Otis Sr.. His son was a good friend of John Adams and had fought against the British Writs of Assistance." Maggie lowered her head. "Unfortunately he was badly injured by someone who thought he was stirring up trouble."

Maggie felt important being able to tell Alex who everyone was. The last time she saw so many members of the Sons of Liberty together, they were dumping the King's tea into the harbor.

"That's William MacKay, a local merchant, and over there the two guys talking to each other are both doctors, Joseph Warren and Thomas Young. Doctor Warren helped me when I had the fever."

Nearly all the main leaders of the Sons of Liberty were here tonight, probably the reason the strangers were targeting this party. One person who hadn't shown up yet was Samuel Adams. John Hancock had returned home about an hour ago and was roaming around the house somewhere. He had said that Samuel was right behind him and on his way. But at this point, there was no sign of him. Alex saw Ben Edes and asked him if he had seen Samuel Adams, but he hadn't. The thought went through both of their minds that perhaps the strangers got to him before the party, but it was too early to jump to that conclusion.

The party was going along very well. Abigail was quite happy, as everyone seemed to be having a good time. There were about forty people there so far, and Abigail thought there would still be about ten more coming. Alex was actually enjoying his time taking glasses of wine and drinks to the guests. He was able to engage in small talk with most everyone at the party that way. Even though, at times, some of the guests were annoyed with the waiter engaging them socially. Twice women came up to Abigail to ask what the waiter thought he was doing. When Abigail told them that Alex was a friend of the family and was earning a little extra money for college, they were more accepting of his casual behavior.

When Alex ran out of drinks from his tray, he went back to the bar to replenish them. Hercules was having a great time serving drinks to the men that had made their way back there. The bar area became a bit of a hangout for the men, who were not quite into all the formalities and social etiquette going on in the front and wanted to relax with a cigar and listen to a few good jokes.

Telling the majority of those jokes was the friendly bartender Hercules Mulligan. It turned out Hercules was a natural at the craft of bartending. He would pour the drinks, take orders, and tell jokes with relative ease. He became so confident that he took a chance, sliding a full ale from one end of the bar to the other without spilling a drop.

On one trip back to the bar, Alex ran into John Hancock, who had heard about Alex through Hercules. The two of them spoke quite a bit about the Sons of Liberty and how things seemed to be coming to the point where the British were determined to get control of Boston and do away with the rebellious group once and for all. John Hancock thought that, if the British were actually coming after the leaders of the Sons of Liberty, it could be a major tipping point in the entire movement.

"If they were successful at cutting the head off the snake, as they called it, it would undoubtedly be a major setback for any sort of changes being made in Boston or the colonies."

Alex agreed but looked at the other side of the coin. "Yet, if the British accumulate all these soldiers in Boston and are unsuccessful in getting the Sons of Liberty under their control, it could be the moral victory needed to convince the rest of the colonies that they could be successful in forcing change."

John Hancock liked Alex's optimism.

"I have no doubts that if the rest of the colonies would join our battle, we could do more than just make changes; we could make our own country."

That was the first time Alex had heard anybody talk about independence from the British. Boston was still very much split between the Patriots and Tories, but a push for independence might be a rallying cry that could bring all the colonies together.

"First things first," John Hancock reminded Alex. "We need to make sure that everybody is safe tonight."

Alex, Maggie, and Hercules all kept a watchful eye throughout the night. They continued to check in with each other to see if anyone was noticing anything suspicious. So far there was no sign of either the strangers or Samuel Adams. Just as Alex was going to suggest that someone go out and look for Samuel Adams, he heard a large ruckus coming from the foyer. When he looked over to the front door, there stood Samuel Adams, chest out and mouth wide open.

"Hey Hancock," he belted out, "you call this a mansion? I have a livestock barn nicer than this!"

Everyone laughed at the obvious sarcasm, and with the arrival of Samuel Adams, there was the sense that now the party had really started. Samuel walked in shaking everyone's hand, sometimes two at a time. If there was any tension in Samuel over the possible attack, you would never have known it. When he got to Abigail, he suddenly stopped and gave her his full attention. He gave a slight bow before her. "How my cousin ever got so fortunate to find a woman as beautiful and enchanting as you, I'll never know."

Used to the attention from Samuel, Abigail smiled and returned the compliment. "Well, my party is officially a success now that you have arrived, dear Samuel."

With nearly all eyes upon him, the unquestioned leader of the Sons of Liberty worked the room like a maestro conducting a symphony. Seeing for himself the devotion everyone had for this leader, Alex knew, above all else, he must keep Samuel Adams safe tonight.

20
A Deadly Toast

The party was rolling along just fine. Alex had never been to a party like this before. Growing up in the islands, he was used to the simple things in life, but now, after having a taste of how the other half lived, Alex knew that he would want more. Maggie was also having the time of her life. She was positively aglow with the music playing, and everyone dressed so elegantly, in such a beautiful home. She might have been holding a tray of appetizers, but in her mind she was the belle of the ball. When she moved about the room from one person to the next, it was as if she were dancing and switching from one partner to the next. Alex had to laugh to himself when he saw Maggie gracefully float across the room. He knew what she was thinking, and he enjoyed watching, as she was lost in the moment.

Alex was also enjoying listening to Samuel Adams. He hadn't the chance to speak to Samuel like he did John Hancock, and he didn't want to interrupt all the fun Samuel was having. Alex was quite certain that Samuel was aware of the dangers of the evening and to reiterate the point wasn't really necessary.

Alex felt like he was part of the conversation with Samuel Adams just the same. When Samuel spoke, he was rarely speaking to an individual person. There was usually a whole group of people that were paying attention to him. Samuel, being conscience of this, spoke loud and in a grand fashion. Alex could follow his conversation from nearly anywhere in the room, as his booming voice resonated from wall to wall.

At one point, he saw Ben Edes talking to Samuel Adams, and Ben pointed over to Alex. Samuel looked over from across the room, and catching Alex's attention, he raised his glass and gave Alex a nod of inclusion. To Alex, that was like a general giving a commendation to a soldier. He nodded back to Mr. Adams and then carried on serving drinks and keeping guard over the party, knowing Samuel Adams and the others were depending on him.

As the night went on, there was a feeling that perhaps it was all a false alarm and that the strangers were not going to show up after all. That all changed when a butler came up to Alex and whispered in his ear. Alex quickly put down his tray and cautiously made his way towards the foyer. Without getting too close, he saw two gentlemen in front of the doorman, who had their invitations in hand. The doorman spotted Alex, and as soon as the strangers turned their back to him and started walking away, he held up the invitations towards Alex and shook his head no – telling Alex that the invitations were forged.

Alex needed confirmation of their identities. He quickly went back to the bar and brought Hercules out to the study. Staying out of sight, they could see the two strangers from a distance. Hercules took a good look at them.

"That's them. I know for sure because the one guy is wearing the suit that I tailored for him."

Hercules looked back at the guy with the suit again and then at Alex.

"It's a shame that such a well-dressed man has to be such a rat."

Alex grabbed Hercules's arm to back him away so that he wouldn't be seen.

"I'm going to warn Ben that they're here. He'll know how to handle them."

Hercules went back to the bar, and Alex found Ben talking to Doc Warren. Alex stood near them, until Ben noticed him, then he motioned to Ben that he needed to talk to him.

Once Ben came over, he whispered, "The two strangers are here."

Ben looked intently at Alex. "Are you sure it's them?"

"Yes, I had Hercules take a good look at them to be sure."

Alex started walking out towards the foyer, coaxing Ben to come with him. Just like with Hercules, Alex pointed the two strangers out. Ben didn't recognize them, and they didn't look like they were itching to do anything at the moment.

"Alex, I want you to keep a careful watch on them and not let them out of your sight."

Alex nodded that he would.

"I'll let Sam and John know about our visitors."

Maggie was walking by and noticed Alex and her father talking. "What's going on?" she asked.

Ben put his hand on her shoulder. "Alex can fill you in, but I want you to be careful and to stay out of danger tonight."

Maggie looked at Alex and back at Ben. "I'll be fine, father."

Alex and Maggie spoke for a moment then went back to serving drinks and hors d'oeuvres, both of them staying close so that they didn't lose track of the two strangers.

At one point, Alex got a bit worried when Maggie bravely went up to them and asked them if they would like anything. Alex couldn't hear what they were saying, but Maggie spoke to them longer than was necessary. A little while later Alex went up to Maggie. "Could you please not fraternize with the enemy?"

Maggie was surprised at such a reaction from Alex. "Oh please, you sound like my father."

Alex looked at her, obviously concerned.

"I'll be fine, Alex, you needn't worry so much."

Alex changed his stance and pretended not to care. "So, did you find out anything?" he asked.

"No, they were pretty tight lipped, but I got the idea that they were definitely up to something."

Alex looked back at the strangers, who had moved into the study, but stayed near the French doors leading to the foyer.

"I wonder where your father and Sam Adams are?"

Just then a maid carrying a full punch bowl and another carrying a tray of glasses came walking into the study with Samuel Adams, John Hancock, and a host of others right behind them. Samuel pointed towards the desk that had been cleared off and told the maids to put the punch bowl and glasses down there.

Alex thought they must be ready to make their ceremonial toast. He walked closer to the desk, where he could see that there were pine needles floating around in the bowl. Alex wondered if people knew that a squirrel had been sniffing around it earlier today, would they still be willing to drink it? Abigail came over and instructed the maids to pour glasses of the pine needle tea. She then spoke up. "It's time for the toast. Any members of the Sons of Liberty that would like to participate are welcome to come up and take a glass of tea."

Alex moved back towards the windows so that he wouldn't be in the way. About ten of the gentlemen in the room came up to the desk and took one of the glasses of tea, including John Adams, Sam Adams, John Hancock, and Ben Edes.

Once it seemed that everyone who wanted a glass had one, Samuel Adams raised his glass of tea and began his speech.

"Friends of America..."

The room fell silent as Samuel spoke.

"Friends of America, we are gathered here tonight with the eyes of the world upon us. They are watching to see if ordinary citizens, whose rights are being taken, can rise up and in one unified voice announce that they have a right to their freedoms and nobody, not even a king, can deprive them of that right."

A mighty "Here, Here!" went up from the crowd.

Alex was still scanning the room and noticed that the two strangers standing by the French glass doors were paying particular attention to the people holding the glasses of tea.

Alex continued to look around. Out of the corner of his eye, he spotted something through the window that caught his attention. Underneath a street lamp, there appeared to be something lying awkwardly on the ground.

Sam Adams continued his toast. "We are here tonight to assure the world that we will fight for those freedoms for as long as it takes."

Another jubilant shout went up.

"Here, Here!"

Alex slowly walked towards the window, trying to make out what was lying there. Then, he saw it, and his heart nearly stopped. Under the lamppost, lying on its back with its tongue hanging out of its mouth and its stiffened legs pointed straight up in the air, was the squirrel. Alex leaned forward and opened his eyes wide. *Sure enough it's the squirrel that was nosing around the tea!*

Samuel Adams finished his speech, "Everyone raise your glasses and drink a toast to our..."

"Stop!" Alex yelled.

"Don't drink the tea!"

Alex started running around the room grabbing people's tea from them. The glasses clinked together, and the tea spilled all over his vest and the floor.

"What's the meaning of this?" Samuel Adams demanded.

"Please sir, put your tea down, and I'll explain."

Samuel instructed the people to put their tea down, and then he looked sternly at Alex. "This better be good," he warned.

With everyone listening for an explanation, Alex swallowed hard and said, "The tea has been poisoned."

The crowd of people became incensed.

"What do you mean *poisoned*?" asked Samuel.

Alex pointed towards the window and started walking towards it. "Look, under the street lamp outside. You'll see a dead squirrel."

The crowd was flabbergasted by the explanation. "So what!" someone yelled out.

Alex suddenly had a moment of doubt when the crowd turned on him, but there was no going back now. "That squirrel was drinking out of the tea as it brewed on the window sill earlier today."

The crowd didn't know quite what to think. Thankfully, Maggie came to his rescue. "I saw it too. The squirrel was sniffing all around the tea."

Sam Adams and John Hancock quickly conferred. John asked Abigail, "Where did the tea come from, Abigail?

Everyone was still listening, stunned by what was transpiring before them.

"The tea arrived at the house before I did. I thought you had ordered it or one of the Daughters of Liberty had dropped it by."

That's when Alex put it all together. "It was the strangers!"

Sam Adams went from confused to intense in a split second. "Where are they?"

Alex pointed towards the doors where they were standing, but nobody was there.

"They're gone!"

Ben Edes headed straight to where they were standing and looked into the foyer. He saw the front door wide open, turned around, and yelled to Sam and John. "They left the house! We might be able to catch them!"

Every able bodied man came running to the foyer and out the front door, including Alex and Hercules, who were raring to go. When they got out to the street, they looked all around, trying to spot the strangers.

"There they go!" Ben yelled, pointing down the road. By the time Alex looked, all he saw was a cloud of dust about three blocks away.

"They escaped," John Hancock lamented.

Sam wasn't convinced. He looked over at two younger men. "George, Thomas, see if you can hunt those two down, and bring them back."

They started heading to their horse when they suddenly realized something, stopped and turned.

"What do they look like?"

Samuel wasn't sure himself.

"I could point them out." Hercules stepped forward like a soldier waiting for his orders.

Samuel slapped Hercules on the back.

"Good man. Take my horse and go with them. Don't waste any time."

Hercules followed the two others who pointed Samuel Adam's horse out to him. They mounted their horses then raced down the road leaving a trail of dust behind them.

Alex watched Hercules take off down the road realizing that they probably weren't going to be able to catch up to the strangers but was a bit envious that Hercules got to be involved in the chase. As they headed back into the house, Alex felt a firm grip on his shoulder and then a friendly arm wrapped around his back. Alex turned his head to the side and saw that it was Samuel Adams who put his arm around him.

"You did a great thing tonight, young man."

Alex felt honored to have helped.

"Thank you, sir." Alex said trying to be as humble as possible.

Sam took his arm off of Alex's shoulder and offered his hand.

"Well, we all owe you a debt of gratitude."

Sam knew that Alex was a man with a bright future.

"What was your name again, he asked."

157

Alex smiled, happy that such an important man was taking such an interest in him.

"Alexander Hamilton, sir."

Samuel gripped Alex's hand warmly with both of his hands.

"You're going to be a great American, Mr. Hamilton. I can just feel it."

Alex stopped and soaked in the moment as everyone walked back into the house. Relieved that everything was fine and nobody got hurt, Alex pondered the tragedy that was averted. John Hancock was probably right, he thought. Things are going to have to go one way or the other pretty soon in Boston. Either the King will get his subjects back under his control, or the colonists will rise up in a revolution. Alex couldn't help but marvel at his circumstance. To think that less than a year ago he was on an island in the West Indies, and now here he was in America witnessing what could be the birth of a new nation.

21
Humble Hero

Back inside, everyone was discussing what had just occurred. All those men who were holding a glass of the poisoned pine needle tea were breathing a heavy sigh of relief. They had eluded a terrible occurrence, and for this, they were thankful.

When Alex walked back into the house, Doctor Young began clapping, and soon the entire party was clapping for Alex and shaking his hand as he walked by. Alex was stunned at the attention and at a loss for words. When the clapping finally simmered down, John Hancock addressed the crowd.

"Everything is under control now, thanks to Mr. Hamilton and his friends. And you can rest assured that we'll be reassessing the security of our organization for the future. But, for tonight, relax and enjoy each other's fellowship. Strike up the band!"

The musicians promptly moved into the parlor and struck up a lively tune. Many people followed the band into the parlor and began dancing on the parquet floor.

As the party quickly picked up where it had left off, Abigail watched with a pleased look on her face. She walked over to Alex and Maggie and invited them to stay as her guests, taking their scarlet work clothes back from them. People continued to come up to Alex the entire night and thank him for what he had done. Alex was starting to feel a little self-conscious about the whole thing.

He watched as Samuel and John continued to speak together, undoubtedly about the night's events. After a little while, Hercules and the two young men returned from their chase, unable to find any trace of the strangers who were long gone. Abigail invited Hercules to join the party and asked for his scarlet vest back, but Hercules didn't want to give it up. He was having a great time as a bartender, so he just went right back to doing it again.

Maggie was enjoying officially being one of the guests. She swayed back and forth to the music as she watched others dance. Alex had thought of a few different ways to ask Maggie to dance but couldn't quite manage to get himself to do it. His palms were getting sweaty, and each time he approached her he chickened out at the last moment.

Maggie noticed how Alex was suddenly turning into a scared schoolboy right before her eyes and tried to help him with his confidence. When the next song started, Maggie cooed in her most suggestive voice, "I love this song," lighting her eyes up with excitement in the universal hint that she wanted to dance. Yet there was still no movement from Alex, who didn't quite pick up on the opening given by Maggie.

Just then, Alex felt a sharp poke in his side and someone whispering in his ear. It was Samuel Adams.

"You know for such a smart guy you sure have a lot to learn about women. Ask her to dance for crying out loud, before someone else does."

Samuel gave him a gentle push towards Maggie causing Alex to awkwardly fall into her. Feeling like he had no other choice, he asked her, "Maggie, would you?"

Before he could even get the words out, Maggie grabbed him by the hand and led him out to the dance floor. She placed one of his hands on her waist and put her hand on his shoulder, and they began to dance.

"That wasn't so hard now, was it?" She asked Alex as they both enjoyed a good laugh. From that point on, they spent the rest of the night laughing and dancing.

22
A Kiss Goodbye

After a good night's sleep, Alex and Hercules were all packed up and ready to hit the road back to New York. They stopped back at the Edes residence to say goodbye to the family and thank them for everything. Ben had given a lot of thought to what happened last night and was weighing his options for his family.

"I fear that things are going to get worse in Boston before they get better." Ben told Alex. "I'm considering moving my family to Watertown until everything cools down."

Alex could understand Ben's concern for the safety of his wife Martha and their ten children.

"What would happen to the Gazette?" Alex asked.

Ben shook his head and smiled. "The press never stops," he answered. "I can move much of the operation to Watertown and still distribute the newspaper back here in Boston."

With Alex going back to New York, Ben wanted to encourage him to write to the newspaper about his experiences.

"Alex, you have a gift that few others possess. It is the obligation of those people who have the ability to lead to take it upon themselves to do just that."

Alex felt the same way and was glad to hear that Ben supported him in that role.

Ben told Alex, "If you send me an article, I'll be sure to publish it in the Gazette. If it strikes a chord with the readers, I'm sure it will get picked up by every paper along the eastern seaboard."

Alex had written a lot of articles that appeared in papers back in Nevis and St. Croix. He once even had a letter published by the *New York Times*. It got him a lot of attention, leading to his eventual scholarship at Kings College. Alex always felt that his writing could be an avenue to move his career forward.

"I'll get started on an article as soon as I get back to college." Alex shook Ben's hand as a promise to send the article. Ben almost forgot one thing.

"Remember to use a pen name. You don't want the wrong people to be upset with whatever you write."

Alex nodded his head. "I'll remember."

Hercules checked that Betsy was securely hitched to the buggy and ready to go. Betsy was well rested and had plenty to eat and drink while she stayed in the Edes' stable.

Alex was hoping to see Maggie this morning before they left, but she was nowhere around. Alex and Hercules said their final goodbyes to the members of the Edes family who had gathered outside to see them off. Mrs. Edes noticed that Alex was looking all around for someone.

"Maggie went to the market this morning. She said she was going to try to get back to say goodbye."

Alex hung his head but then remarked. "No need to worry, if you could just tell her I said goodbye, I would appreciate it."

Alex grabbed a hold of the buggy and pulled himself up onto the seat. Hercules got on the other side and gave two quick whistles to Betsy, who began to pull the Buggy forward. Alex continued to look around for Maggie to no avail. Hercules and Alex waved to the family as they pulled away and headed down the street.

About half way down the block, Hercules heard a faint shout in the distance.

"Wait! Wait!"

It was Maggie running down the street after them. Hercules pulled on Betsy's reigns and brought the buggy to a stop. In no time, Maggie caught up to them and, without hesitation, leaped up towards Alex, who caught her in his arms. She gave him a big hug, looked him in his eyes, and gave him a quick and tender kiss.

Alex was stunned and didn't move. Maggie leaned back and allowed herself to step back down from the buggy.

"Don't you forget about me, Alexander Hamilton," Maggie said.

From the goofy look on Alex's face, that was pretty much a guarantee. To spare his friend from saying anything stupid and leaving with some dignity, Hercules gave two quick whistles, and they were on their way. As they moved down the road, Alex still had that goofy look on his face, with half a smile and his eyes a glaze. Hercules saw him and punched him in the shoulder.

"Ouch, what did you do that for?" Alex complained.

"Just trying to bring you back down to earth, buddy."

Alex rubbed his shoulder knowing he deserved it.

Winding through the crooked streets of Boston, Alex noticed how different the city appeared to him compared to when they first arrived. Having met so many of the citizens and having seen so many of the atrocities the British inflicted upon them, Alex was now firmly on the side of the Boston patriots. He decided, at that point, that he would do everything that he could to support the cause of freedom.

Just as they got through the edge of town, they saw a familiar rider approaching them from the opposite direction. It was Paul Revere returning from his trip to New York. Hercules brought Betsy to a stop and waved his arms to flag down Paul Revere. Pulling back the reins of his horse, Paul Revere stopped amongst a cloud of dust.

"Gentlemen, we meet again."

Hercules was glad that Paul Revere had remembered them.

"I trust that you found Ben Edes and got your message to the Sons of Liberty."

Alex wanted to tell Paul Revere all about it but thought there was almost too much to tell.

"Yes, we found Mr. Edes and everything worked out in the end."

Alex didn't want to tell the whole story, figuring he'd probably would hear about it from his Sons of Liberty friends soon enough.

"How about you, Mr. Revere, how did you fare in New York?"

Alex remembered that he had gone to New York to try to garner support for the people of Boston. After seeing the need first hand, Alex was hopeful that Paul Revere was successful.

"Excellent. There is more empathy for Boston than I had even anticipated. It seems as if the people of New York have realized that if the British could clamp down on Boston,

166

what's to say that they couldn't do the same to New York next?"

Alex knew that a lot of things that happened in Boston had happened in New York soon after. In fact, the New York Sons of Liberty had their own version of a tea party dumping the Kings tea into New York Harbor. Throughout the colonies, the rumblings of liberty were simmering just under the surface, ready to follow Boston's lead and rise up in defense of freedom.

"There's more encouraging news," remarked Paul Revere. "There is a calling for a meeting to take place in Philadelphia between representatives of all the colonies to discuss what actions the colonies should take as a whole in this conflict. They want to call this group of delegates the Continental Congress."

Alex thought the idea was fantastic. "That is exactly what is needed." Alex enthusiastically told Revere. "We will be a much more persuasive force as a cohesive group than we ever could be as a single colony."

Paul Revere couldn't agree more. "Let's hope that the rest of the colonies are as supportive of the alliance as our two colonies."

With that statement, Paul Revere tipped his hat, reared his horse up on it hind legs, leaned forward in his saddle, and took off down the road as if he was shot from a cannon. Hercules just watched in amazement.

"That guy sure knows how to make an exit."
Alex laughed as Betsy slowly began pulling
the buggy down the road.

23
Alex the Patriot

The trip back to New York was relaxing. They had good weather the whole way and didn't run into any thieves who often prey upon vulnerable travelers. Alex had plenty of time to think about everything that had happened. He felt like it was his destiny that he came to America and became involved with a budding revolution. He would continue to carry out that destiny by taking a leadership role in the cause, and maybe someday he could be a delegate representing New York in a convention like Paul Revere spoke of.

Alex had spent a lot of time reading about history and the great civilizations of the past. In each case, greatness was achieved when circumstances presented opportunity and men were brave enough to embrace the challenges and create something that was better. America was at that point, where greatness could emerge from opportunity, and Alex felt destined to be a leader in the cause.

Once back at Kings College, Alex resumed the life of a student. Yet he also looked for opportunities to lead. He followed the activities of the New York Sons of Liberty, he became popular for his rousing speeches on campus, and he wrote articles in support of the patriots for the school newspaper.

When he heard word that the Continental Congress had actually formed and met in Philadelphia, Alex decided that it was time to write his article and send it to Ben. The article supported the brave men of the Continental Congress and was given tremendous reviews. He sent it to Ben Edes at the *Boston Gazette* and to James Rivington at the *New York Gazetteer*. The article eventually became a pamphlet supporting the cause and was distributed throughout the colonies.

Alex remembered Ben's advice not to put his name on the article so that the British wouldn't know who wrote it. After some careful thought over what to use as his pen name, he decided to borrow the phrase Samuel Adams used to start his toast to the Sons of Liberty. At the bottom of his article Alex signed,

A friend of America.

What Happened Next

On April 18th, 1775, Paul Revere galloped through the Massachusetts countryside yelling the memorable words, "The British are coming! The British are coming!" The Revolutionary War had begun with the battles of Lexington and Concord. The following year, on July 4th, 1776, Thomas Jefferson penned the Declaration of Independence, giving birth to the United States of America.

As war waged on, General George Washington, of the Continental Army, needed to hire a soldier to be his top assistant, or Aide-de-Camp. For the prestigious position, Washington chose a young man fresh out of King's College named Alexander Hamilton. When George Washington went on to become the new nation's first President, he named Alexander Hamilton to the important cabinet position of Secretary of Treasury.

Hamilton is largely recognized as the main architect in forming the economic framework for the United States. By becoming one of America's founding fathers, Alexander Hamilton was able to realize his destiny.

Images of Alexander Hamilton

Alex Hamilton at age 15

Hamilton on the ten dollar bill

Acknowledgements

Cover
Alexander Hamilton saving King's College from a patriotic mob, 1775. Hand colored woodcut of a Howard Pyle illustration, 1884. North Wind Picture Archives

Page vii
Map of Revolutionary Boston, Brian Schmit, 2012

Page 18
Join or Die, Benjamin Franklin, The Pennsylvania Gazette, May 9, 1754. Library of Congress

Page 51
John Adams, Coat of Arms, Brian Schmit, 2012

Page 79
Destruction of Tea at Boston Harbor, Currier and Ives Foundation, 1846. Library of Congress

Page 100
The Bloody Massacre perpetrated in Kings Street Boston on March 5th, 1770 by a party of the 29th rgt. Paul Revere engraved 1770. Library of Congress

Page 175
A. Hamilton, drawn from life, Jan 11, 1773. Artist unknown. Library of Congress